DEATH OF A TRANSVESTITE

Also by Ed Wood, Jr.

Hollywood Rat Race
Killer in Drag

DEATH OF A
TRANSVESTITE
by Ed Wood, Jr.

Four Walls Eight Windows
New York /London

© 1999 Estate of Edward D. Wood, Jr.

Published in the United States by
Four Walls Eight Windows
39 West 14th Street, room 503
New York, NY 10011
http://www.fourwallseightwindows.com

U.K. offices:
Four Walls Eight Windows/Turnaround
Unit 3 Olympia Trading Estate
Coburg Road, Wood Green
London N22 6TZ

First edition published in 1967 by Pad Library. British
Commonwealth edition published by Gorse in 1995. Four Walls
Eight Windows edition published in 1999.

Library of Congress Cataloguing-in-Publication Data:
Wood, Edward D. (Edward Davis), 1924-1978.
    [Let me die in drag]
    Death of a transvestite / by Edward D. Wood, Jr.
                    p.   cm.
    Published: Let me die in drag. London : Gorse.
    Sequel to: Killer in drag.
    ISBN 1-56858-121-1
    I. Title.
    PS3573.05925L48   1999
    813'.54—dc21
                    98-49259
                    CIP
10 9 8 7 6 5 4 3 2 1
Printed in Canada

Although Edward D. Wood, Jr. was his legal and preferred name,
the author was also known as Ed Wood, Jr. or Edw. D. Wood, Jr.

CHAPTER ONE

INTRODUCTION TO FATE

We entered Glen Marker's cell, a bleak, cold arrangement of bars and solid cement, at seven-thirty p.m. It wasn't a pleasure visit, and even as we entered the cell Glen could be seen visibly shaken by the finality of our presence.

The same situation hadn't happened in several years—that a man was to be executed in the State electric chair in our eastern city. But the facts were all in and any last minute appeals had been completely exhausted. There was to be no executive clemency. Glen already had a small spot shaved in the back of his once curly black hair. A shaved spot which would in a few short hours be attached with electrodes.

I looked down to the former top Syndicate killer and considered the crimes for which he had been condemned. The slight young man was apparently resigned to his judged fate. Naturally he wasn't overjoyed at the prospect, but then he wasn't crying about it either. For a time, in the past, Glen had thought he'd escaped justice forever—as in all such cases, it was a fool thought.

"How was your night?" I spoke in dry tones; not unpleasant, but official.

Glen grinned at me. "Got a cigarette, Warden?" I produced the cigarette but the uniformed turnkey lit it for him. He let the smoke drift up around his head. "Want me to say fine, the hotel service is great?"

"You're the star of this show, Glen. I suppose you can say just about anything you want."

"Why do you guys do it?" Glen's eyes were solid.

"That's all according to what you're referring to."

"A year ago I was so shot up it was a miracle anybody could put me back together again. All that patching just so I'd live to see the inside of your little green room. Wouldn't it have been better, and less expensive, to let me pass out of the scene while I was blacked out and going fast? All those doctors, the hospitals, the cops and courts, the extradition across the country... seems to me everything could have been so much more simple the other way."

"The State must always attempt to claim its own."

"What kind of an answer is that?"

"Stock."

"That figures." Glen drew on the last of the cigarette, then crushed it out on the cement floor with the toe of his felt slipper. "Stock answers seem to be a format for all things in this world."

I shrugged.

Glen grinned. "That's another stock bit—the old shrug. The loss of words. The fall of realistic communication. The non-commital." He leaned back against the cold, bleak wall, still grinning. "Warden, I've lived in a realistic world all my life. There were no stock answers—no ifs, ands or buts—it was all fact. When I was issued a contract, the subject of that contract was as good as dead the minute I hung up the phone. There were no stock answers to my subjects. Oh, I suppose they had lots of questions, only they couldn't talk me out of what I had to do, so why waste the time listening? Now I find myself in the position of my subjects and I have a lot of the same questions and I don't get anything but stock answers. It makes me want to laugh." And he did.

"Let's figure it this way, Glen. Maybe there are times when only stock answers are the answers."

"Like right now."

I nodded my head. "There are certain things you must be told... from the regulations."

"I'd bet you've got regulations for everything—except how a man must take his own demise."

"Are you planning to give us trouble, Glen?" His tone troubled me.

"Far from it. Not in the least. Not a bit. You've got all the power on your side." He paused, then looked directly into my eyes. "Tell me something, Warden—without your usual stock answers."

"If I can."

"You can if you want." Glen indicated he wanted another cigarette and he waited until the lighting procedure had been completed before he spoke again. "Is it true, after I'm strapped in and hooded—the second before you pull the switch— one of your men will smash my testicles?"

I'm sure the shock showed plainly on my face as I looked to the others. I wished the padre was with us but there was no man of the cloth in the cell as Glen had requested.

9

"What gave you an idea like that?" I sputtered, after the first shock subsided.

"Sounds logical, doesn't it? At least it does to me. In the Oriental countries, if a guy has a headache they stick pins in his ass—transferring the pain so to speak—wherever the hurt is more painful at that particular time. But to answer your question more directly. I've met a few guys who spent some time on death row and escaped the eventual big show—even got out of prison finally. One of them, after getting off the row, served another five years as assistant to the prison Medical Examiner. He was present at the autopsy of thirty-two executed men. Electrocuted men. Every one of them, according to this man, had crushed balls."

"You can rest assured no such thing occurs."

"Can I?"

"Of course. First of all there are witnesses to every execution, some of whom the condemned man requests himself."

"I'd thought of that. But there would be ways if you wanted... perhaps a trap in the seat itself."

"That's unthinkable."

"Sure, I couldn't agree more. However, from your tone, something does it. Am I right?"

"If such a crushing exists, and I'm not admitting it does, it's because of certain constrictions to the body as the electric currents pass through. There would be honest medical reasons for the condition, reasons I am not qualified to explain, and reasons with which, at such a time, you should not be concerning yourself."

Glen laughed a short burst. "Not concern myself? If I shouldn't concern myself at such a time, who should?"

One of the guards, my turnkey, spoke up almost fatherly. "Take it from me, Glen—and you know I wouldn't steer you wrong—there's nothing to it."

Glen glanced across to the uniformed turnkey.

"Okay, Uncle Charlie. I'll take your word—for now! After all, it won't be long before I find out firsthand, will it?" Glen inhaled deeply from the cigarette. "We'll let the whole thing drop." Then he quickly changed the subject. "I understand I do have some sort of distinction in this whole mess, however?"

I nodded. "The pickets against capital punishment have been parading in front of the main gate since noontime. Hundreds of them."

"The first person to go in your chair for," he cocked his head, "how long has it been?"

"Six years."

"Well now. That is some kind of a record. Somebody must have really had the finger in after me."

"Remember a guy named Rance Dillon?" I lit one of my own cigarettes as I spoke.

"Sure. The court said I put some holes in him. What they didn't like to point up was what an ass-grabbing louse he was. He made sure he had his finger in every racket in the state. Only the Syndicate didn't like it when he didn't turn over their cut. They don't approve of such things as that. Let one get away with it and they'll all try, then where would any kind of an organization be?"

"Be that as it may. But what you don't seem to know is he was the Governor's brother-in-law. Now maybe you do realize how much pressure is put on the Governor by other state officials. Then add to that how much pressure his wife could put on him, against you, when it was you who took her brother's life."

"Guess nobody could fight against those odds."

"Nobody!"

Glen, as before, crushed the cigarette out on the cement floor with the toe of his felt slipper. "Remember what I said before—about your regulations and how they cover everything except how a man takes his own death?"

"I took no offense by the remark."

"How could you? There was no offense intended! I was merely referring in my mind, to a pointed conversation the killer and I had during our shoot-out back in Hollywood that last night."

"I don't understand."

"You couldn't, Warden! You weren't there! And it's about things that didn't come out during the trial. Why should I have told that story and added more fuel to their already blazing furnaces?"

"And you want to tell something now?"

Glen shrugged. "What harm can it do now? Besides, isn't it the old saying, 'confession is good for the soul'?"

"Do you want a priest, Glen?"

"I'm not a Catholic. No, I won't need any representative of the hereafter. Besides, I don't

12

think it would do my case any more good there than it would have in court. No... no... you and old Uncle Charlie there and your other men, you're all that's necessary..." He stopped abruptly. "How much time is left?"

"Three hours."

"Just about time enough to read a novel." Glen grinned. "That is if one reads fast enough." The grin was short-lived. "I've got a last request I suspect?"

I gave my official nod again. "Anything within reason." I kept my voice quiet, but there was a definite attempt at being official. I felt something about the other man's words whereby I wanted to hear more.

"Again the regulations—always the screwin' regulations! And I'd bet my last request isn't covered by any of your regulations."

"That would have to be pretty far-out!"

"I've always been a pretty far-out character."

"I'd say that's on the record. You had quite a gimmick going for you."

"I finally tried to get out—get away from the Syndicate. That's why they sent another killer after me. I was a KILLER IN DRAG, so it was only natural they sent another drag to kill me. They figured I knew too much about them to live. You've got to give the Syndicate a lot of credit—it's not run by a bunch of schnooks and dunderheads. They are brains all the way down the line. Figure the facts. I'm a transvestite, so they send another of my kind after me. It's the only way I could have been tracked down—only another drag could think the way I would—know the kind of places I'd eventually go. Guess that sort of makes

13

me the stupid one, doesn't it?"

"You've dressed that way a long time?"

"So my mother told me, God rest her soul. Long before I have any memory. I guess you have to put it down as girls' clothing has been my first love since before I can remember."

"There's a great number of men, known and unknown, running around wearing girls' clothes who haven't taken up a gun. Laws are pretty liberal these days about what someone should wear or not wear. You took up a gun and used your transvestite desires as a cover."

"The gun was simply a means to quick, easy cash. A lot of cash. Do you know I got five grand a contract, and not once was I tagged by the cops for any of the contracts? Until this last time. Even that wasn't for a contract. An old man got murdered by his homosexual lover, and I'm tapped for the thing simply because I was in the room." Glen grinned sardonically. "Once I was brought back for that investigation —simply a word into the District Attorney's ear by those who wanted me out of the way and all the rest of it fell into place. Which gets me to the request. My last request. It's not for a big, special supper as I suspect all your 'go out's' have wanted in the past. The foremost thought in any honest transvestite's mind is to die in female attire."

My eyes flashed to the guards then back to Glen as he continued. "And to be buried in such clothes. That's my last request, Warden. I want you to get me a blouse, a soft cardigan sweater, a skirt, high-heeled shoes and the proper undies. And don't tell me regulations forbid it

14

because I doubt if such a request has ever been made before, so there can't be any regulations for a precedent."

I was shocked into speechlessness. It was true, I never had such a request. There was no precedent to make any decisions by. But I was top man in the prison. The whole thing would be up to me for a decision.

Glen spoke up again as if reading my thoughts. "You're top dog around here, Warden. All you have to do is say yes. Besides! What should it really matter to you what I'm wearing when I go out—as long as I go out? Of course, the witnesses and the press might make something of it all later on. But you can always stand on the last request routine. How can you refuse such a simple last request?"

"That really isn't the point. I suppose there's no harm in it. But we don't have any clothing like that around here. This is a man's prison. Maybe a couple of old prison dresses left over from the old days, but nothing as fine as you've described."

"Tell you what," Glen persisted. "Let's make a deal. You find what I so desperately need and I fill you in completely about my Hollywood escapades. Now there's a real feather in your cap. Nobody's gotten that story out of me all the way through this thing. I would have gone to my grave with the story untold, and I will if you don't go along with the gag."

"I guess everybody connected with this thing would like to hear that story of yours. But it's just about impossible to get the things in time. There wouldn't be a store open in fifty or more miles at this time of the night. It's just out of the question."

"And *I* won't settle for some old prison dress."

The guard whom Glen had referred to as Uncle Charlie moved in close to me. "Pardon me, Warden. But maybe I might be able to help. You know my oldest daughter is just about his size. She's always buying clothes and don't wear half of them. Shoes—sizes I mean—might be the only problem. But I reckon he could squeeze into them. He won't have far to walk."

I thought for a long, silent moment as my eyes traveled from Glen to Charlie, then back to Glen again. Finally my mind was made up. I certainly wanted the story. Then I could really lord it over those who could not get it out of the condemned man. "By God, Charlie, I'll go for it! Your place is just outside the South Gate. Shouldn't take you fifteen minutes."

"Better say half an hour. I may have a little trouble explaining what it's all about to the kid..."

"Make it as fast as you can. And bring the tape recorder from my office."

Glen leaned back. His fondest desires were to be fulfilled.

*****

WARDEN'S NOTE

I taped Glen's story in its entirety but the holes he couldn't fill firsthand left much to be desired. However, what he had related so intrigued me. I decided to follow through as far

16

as possible to get all the facts—to search this man down. The only way to accomplish that was to trace each of the people he had been intimate with during his West Coast escapade.

Then, in a last step, each of their stories had to be put into proper sequence, as they happened, until the complete character and story of the man himself could be exposed.

We take exceptional notice of the fact that, on the tape, when Glen talks of Glenda he speaks of her in second person, but when he refers to Glen it is always with the first person I.

CHAPTER TWO

L.A. POLICE REPORT #794—AIRPORT EMPLOYEES

The Killer got off the jet airliner from New York at Los Angeles International Airport: a tall, extremely thin, shapeless man in his early twenties. He had a hawk-like nose: the only distinguishing characteristic impossible to deny. And it was to this nose the foul, sour-egg odors of the Los Angeles smog presented itself. The Killer screwed up that nose at the faint smell, and couldn't help but marvel at those Californians he had suddenly become involved with, who seemed to take it as a natural, everyday occurrence.

Since he was the last to disembark from the airliner, he took a long pause, standing just outside the hatch. The mechanical canopied ramp had long since been moved into place, and it was difficult to see any terrain beyond.

It had been an interesting sight from the air, all the night lights of the great expanse of the city—a drive-in movie, where the cartoon ending with "That's All Folks!" spread across the giant screen, visible even at that altitude. The fantastic high-rise hotel which rested on the very edge of the airport, and more so, the vastness of the airfield itself—the blue, smog-cutting lights which indicated the runway. The Killer marveled at the sight. He wanted to see it more clearly...

He walked the length of the mechanical ramp, the disgusting smell of jet fuel invading that hawk-nose along with the smog and other fumes.

The Killer liked the sights of the airport he had witnessed from the air, but the stench on the ground—that was another matter!

N.Y. POLICE FILE #OIO—HARRY 'THE MOUSE' KIMBOY

Just under five hours ago he had been in New York City in a place, a dive called Jake's Place. He had been wearing a green jersey dress under a light coat; his brunette wig had been a bit straggly due to the urgent nature of the call, and not enough time to get it property prepared. The Mouse, a Syndicate runner, had given him a name. That name was top on the list for extinction... GLEN MARKER, HOLLYWOOD. The Mouse had given him a picture of Glen as he looked as a man, and Glenda as he looked as a girl. A Syndicate killer who did his extermination duties dressed in female attire.

"I don't like you, and I don't like none of yer kind," The Mouse had said.

"Jam it up your gigi," the Killer had thrown back at him. "Just give me the cash money, runt." And with a deepest venom his words sunk in.

The Mouse had started to stand up. He was stopped by the low, pointed words of the Killer. "Sit down, Mouse..." The Mouse sank back to his chair. He took a large envelope from his pocket and shakily slid it across the table.

"Your fee and tickets," said The Mouse nervously.

L.A. POLICE REPORT #794—AIRPORT EMPLOYEES

That had been nearly five hours before. Then the jet trip from New York to California, following the setting sun across the continent.

There was a job to be done—a job he liked. The Killer intensely liked his job of death-dealing.

After finding his luggage had not been delivered to the dock as yet, he made his way up the escalator to the airport lounge where he ordered a whiskey and soda, and took a long time to drink it... a very long time, as he looked out to the airport activity beyond and his mind began to wander.

N.Y. POLICE FILE #960—TEXAS LOUIS— SYNDICATE MEMBER

It had been the theory of the Syndicate: it takes one to know one. Thus he had been hired for the job. But what a job it would be. Los Angeles was a big city. This would be like trying to find the proverbial needle in the haystack. And even after he found him, Glen was not going to be an easy bit of work. Glen had been the top Syndicate drag killer until he had pulled out for parts unknown. Even the widespread tentacles of the Syndicate couldn't trace him, until a girl he had befriended in the

Midwest turned up in the big Island City looking for an old girlfriend of Glen's. She had been persuaded to reveal all she knew... the story of how he had escaped two crooked highway patrolmen who had been finally killed in a crash. Now he was on his way to Los Angeles, driving a small grey convertible which he had purchased in Colorado.

"What was he wearing?" A hard-faced man with a jagged scar along the side of his cheek hit the already battered girl once more across the mouth. A new rush of blood splattered from her cut lips.

It took the girl a moment to let her senses swim back into focus before she could answer. "They call me Red," she whimpered.

He hit her again—a resounding blow to the side of her head. The impact sent her sprawling to the dirty waterfront warehouse floor. Two of the other pug-uglies roughly picked her up once more and slammed her back into the chair. "I don't care what in hell you're called, you're just another bitch to me! I asked what in hell the bastard was wearing when he left Colorado!"

Rose, Red's real name, didn't cry easily, but the tears suddenly began to flow in a torrent across her torn, pained face. Glen had been kind to her. However, she knew her life was at stake... toughs like these played for keeps. She'd met muscle all her life, but nothing like the vicious creeps who were assaulting her now. She staggered her words through broken, bleeding lips and teeth. "Red."

"Red what?"

"That's what I'm trying to tell you, if you'll

stop using my head for a punching bag long enough to let me."

"Spit it out, broad!"

"Glen was kind to me. I helped him get away from a couple of crooked fuzz... everybody called me Red because I always wore red. Everything I owned, from the skin out, head to toe red. Everybody in town could tell me from a long way off. Glen became Glenda, wearing one of my red outfits: sweater, slacks, raincoat and beret."

"Where was he going?"

"He... he... Glen was going to Los Angeles."

L.A. POLICE REPORT #766 AIRPORT EMPLOYEES

The darkness and the departure whistle of the Queen Mary blended together to hide her piercing scream, as her tied, weighted body was dropped into the East River.

The Killer snapped back to the present as a big jet roared its motors for take-off. He ordered a second drink, but this one he gulped down, then left the airport lounge.

L.A. POLICE REPORT #795—LUKE WALTERS — TAXI DRIVER

After he picked up his luggage he hailed a taxi cab and was started on his long, hectic trip on the freeway toward the Strader Motel, a Syndicate-owned motel on the Sunset Strip in Hollywood.

It would be his place of operation. The Syndicate wanted it this way, so that's the way it would be. And Glen Marker, or Glenda Satin, as he seemed to prefer being called, was marked by the Syndicate for death, and *that's* the way it would be.

CHAPTER THREE

BASED ON TAPE CONFESSION

Glenda had made only one stop before reaching the Colorado State line—a gas station some fifty miles from the mountains. The siren had long since given up the chase, but Glenda was not to be fooled by that old ruse. Sooner or later a roadblock would be set up, then the trouble would start. Her red outfit was a dead giveaway. Mac and Ernie weren't about to let her get out of the state—not with what she knew. The radio was a fast medium, but already fifty miles or more... where were the road blocks? This was the only highway. There had been no side roads until a mile or two back, only mountain roads and cliffs.

Glenda took off her red wig and fluffed out the auburn hair. It was time for a change, but she couldn't become Glen at that point. It might startle the old gas station attendant into jumping right for his phone. Glenda must remain for a time yet—but a change of clothing was in order, and immediately. It had been a lucky move she'd made, putting her suitcase into the trunk of the car before she left the carnival. There was a good selection of Glenda's clothing in it. She'd have no trouble in changing her outward appearance.

She was thus engrossed as the old man leaned in at the window. "Afternoon."

"Fill it up." Glenda's beautiful red-lipped smile and musical voice stirred something deep in the old man.

He walked, suddenly stiff-legged, to the ancient pump and took down the hose. Glenda made a big show of her ankles protruding a bit below the red slacks—well-turned ankles, slim, above the high-heeled red pumps. "Do you have a ladies' room?"

The old man winked at her. "Only one—for both," then he quickly added, "but they's a lock on the inside so's you won't be disturbed none." He cackled at what he thought was a joke.

"Thank you." The music in her voice again caused the old attendant to tense up.

Glenda moved to the trunk and unlocked it. She started to take out her thick suitcase.

"You come down the mountain road?"

She paused for one dangerous moment, then silently looked back to the suitcase.

"You must have," the old man cackled. "No other way."

Glenda slammed the trunk shut. She was holding the heavy suitcase. The old man put the hose back on the pump, still unused. "That looks too heavy for a pretty thing like you to carry." He took the suitcase from her hand and started to lead the way across to a building at the rear of the station, which itself was little more than a shack.

Glenda was cautious. "Why did you mention the mountain road ?"

"Thought maybe you see'd the big crash-up back yonder."

"No. What was it all about?" A very calm

Glenda.

"Two highway cops crashed into a circus wagon. Went right over the cliff—killed 'em both."

"Killed?" Glenda's throat went suddenly dry.

"Somethin' wrong? You look sick."

Glenda composed herself quickly. "No, I'm alright. I do so much driving, I get nauseous when I hear about highway accidents and deaths."

The old attendant set the suitcase down in front of the shack. He indicated the door with a grin. "There she be. Ain't nothin' fancy like the big places, but they's runnin' water an' an old mirror. I'll get ya a cold soda-pop. Might rightly fix ya up yer not feelin' so good."

"That's very kind of you." Glenda picked up her suitcase and entered the shack outhouse.

So Ernie and Mac were dead. Glenda had been a Syndicate killer, but she held respect for the real law enforcement officers—after all, they had a job to do the same as Glenda did her job. But when a cop turned rotten, it turned her stomach. Ernie and Mac were rotten to the core. Let them rot in hell. The world was better off without them... the bastards! Let them rot in HELL! Yet they'd probably go down in history as heroes, and be buried with all policemen's honors. And the ever-lovin' taxpayers would undoubtedly get stuck with paying somebody a pension for them for life. It's always happened that way. An honest guy gets kicked in the teeth and a rat gets fat. Glenda vowed to herself that she would write a letter, anonymous of course, divulging their true characters. Probably no one would believe it, but she'd know the satisfaction of doing it all the same.

Glenda stripped to her bra and panties, and had just taken out the long-sleeved, turtleneck white angora slipover sweater and blue velvet skirt, along with a pink nylon slip, as the light knock came on the shack door.

"Yes?"

"Mr. Perkins."

"Who?"

"I got your soda-pop here."

"Oh—just a minute." She started to take up a thin pink negligee from the suitcase, but in the move she caught sight of her lovely frame in the cracked mirror. A broad grin crossed her face. "Why not?" she said silently. The grin became broader.

Glenda turned to the door, threw back the hook and opened the door. Her brassiere-and-panty-clad body confronted the old man, a sight she was sure he hadn't seen in years, if ever. He would have dropped the soda-pop if Glenda hadn't taken it quickly from his hand. "Thank you," she said in her most sexy voice, and slowly, softly closed and hooked the shack door again.

The soft moan of withheld, long-stagnated lust came from beyond the door and caused Glenda to laugh silently as she let the thin nylon slip drift down over her head and into smooth lines about her body. Then came the blue velvet skirt followed by the luscious white angora sweater.

The season wasn't violently cold, but it was cool enough to warrant the interesting warmth of the clothing she wore, and as she packed the red raincoat, red sweater, slacks and high-heeled

27

pumps, Glenda couldn't help but think back to Rose Graves. What a lay! He caressed the soft wool of the red sweater. The fragrance of Red's heavy perfume was still strong. Not only was Red a good lay, everything in bed, but Red had helped Glen when he needed it most, against the heaviest of odds imaginable. Glenda hoped the money Glen had given Rose would take her a long way from the environment she had been forced into by circumstances. Rose was a good kid—she had a lot of life ahead of her. She'd do well in New York. Barbara would help her get some kind of start in the big city.

Glenda adjusted the nylons to her garter-belt, then slipped her dainty feet into high-heeled black pumps.

She was ready to meet the outside world again. A hostile world, with dark passages concealing things and elements of the shadows and unseen dangers. Even the daylight seemed to hold no safety. When Glen had broken with the Syndicate, the nights and the days had become one thing only—TERROR! He had known his plight, but went along with all the prospects, and there were still many nights that the faces of his victims invaded his subconscious to haunt, to harrass him. There was a time he could have cried all the way to the bank. There became a time he cried for the plight of his victims.

A tremendous black widow spider came out of the woodwork and started across the floor toward Glen's suitcase. Glenda's foot squashed it to death in one swift movement. Death was all around her. She felt it even more so as she looked to the slimy mess of the spider on the floor after her foot had left it. The spider had been the first thing Glen/Glenda had killed since leaving the Syndicate. But death followed him like the deep shadow of disaster it was. The old fag Dalton Van Carter and his Negro servant in New York... all those people at the carnival when the Ferris wheel had collapsed... even Mac and Ernie... where would it all end? Death was always present, only waiting for a time and a place to activate itself. The activation had been manifested in so many ways those past months.

Glenda used the toe of her shoe to viciously kick the remains of the spider back toward the wall from where it had emerged, then snapped the locks on her suitcase and left the shack.

The old attendant turned from filling the gas tank of her car as Glenda came out of the outhouse shack. She went immediately to the trunk and unlocked it, shoving her suitcase far back in.

"I put some oil and water in the front end. Kinda' needed it!" wheezed the old man.

Glenda turned to him. She didn't want to sound surly, but the thoughts of the past caused a deep tone of hatred in her voice. "How much?"

The musical voice was no longer there; the female tones had not disappeared, but there was a despair the old man would never understand. He no longer had a stiff leg as he moved to check his scrawled notations on a tattered pad near the ancient pump. He looked back to the beautiful girl in the angora sweater when he spoke again. "Four-thirty."

Glenda moved the righthand door of her car, opened it, and reached in the glove compartment. She pulled out a wallet and extracted a five dollar bill which she gave to the old man. "Keep it!"

COLORADO POLICE INTERVIEW #1131—
JIM RIVERS—STATION ATTENDANT

The old man grunted. The musical voice of the beautiful thing he had seen in the pink panties and pink-titty holder wasn't there any longer. He didn't feel, any longer, the sensations in his aged groin. "Ah, what the hell?" he muttered. "Just another pussy-shower..." Then he folded the five dollar bill and put it in his dungaree pocket as he started toward the outhouse shack. He couldn't help but think: "Maybe she left something in there I kin remember her by..." His step quickened, his leg once more stiff in anticipation.

CHAPTER FOUR

WARDEN'S NOTE

Rose 'Red' Graves had long since died at the hands of the Syndicate members. Therefore, except for the direct testimony of Barbara Benton, who did so to save her own neck from a murder indictment, we can only search out Rose's thoughts from of composite of many. Basically, there is Glen's own information, which is on the tape. And there are bits of information supplied by other individuals during the investigation.

COMPOSITE REPORT #1—ROSE 'RED' GRAVES

She didn't want to die, but it was apparent she was going to. She screamed, a piercing sound. However, it was drowned out by a boat whistle. The next sound was as she splashed loudly into the black waters of the East River, the heavy weights pulling her naked body quickly downward to the bottom. She tried to scream again, only to have her mouth fill with the cold black water. Panic seized her. She fought desperately to hold her breath—it was as if self-preservation in the form of rememberance was fighting just as desperately to save her.

The picture became as clear to her as if she

were once more reliving the times... she was at the station waiting for her bus when she saw the late papers and their bold headlines. She couldn't believe her eyes. She bought a copy and took it to a bench.

She glanced at the headlines telling of Mac and Ernie's sudden demise. She had to cross her legs tightly to keep her urine intact in her bladder, as it was about to drain out with the joy of the news. She read the article which followed the headlines with even more vigor. She let her hands, on top of her red skirt, caress the inside of her legs—a joy of sexual satisfaction, a climax finally coming over her—the inside of her legs where both Ernie and Mac had been... but never before had she climaxed at their hands or even at the thought of them. On that bus waiting bench, she climaxed... her thighs heaved... her eyes closed in the ecstasy of the pleasurable moment. Her passionately red lips pressed themselves into a kiss, a kiss given to an unseen spectre. And when it was over she stood up, letting the newspaper fall to the bench beside her. She made her way to the ladies' room and there changed the stained red panties she had on. Panties was one thing she carried plenty of. At one time she never knew just when they would need changing quickly. At that point there still was no real change in her life. She had to still make a living. There were always men in the world who would need a girl, and she was available. She loved Glen/Glenda with all her heart. But also in her heart she knew she would never see him again.

She looked into the mirror. The excitement of the moment past, her panties once more clean and dry, she smiled in self-satisfaction. Then thoughts of Glen suddenly and deeply overtook her. "Glenda," she whispered, and she could hear the rain outside the washroom window, and wondered where he was. How had he escaped those crooked cops Mac and Ernie? Had he been instrumental in their departure from this world? How far had her red slacks, sweater, shoes, raincoat and beret taken him?

Rose was thus engrossed when the departure of her bus for New York was announced over the loudspeaker. She quickly dropped her dirtied red panties into a trash can, grabbed up her suitcase, and moments later the bus was carrying her toward the big Island City of New York.

At first she was fascinated by the sights along the way, until the drone of the motor seemed to lull her into a sleepy stupor. She tried to fight it because there was so much to see. It was her first trip of any great length, but she couldn't fight the inevitable.

During the thousand or more miles, her mind went back to Glen/Glenda many times—to their first meeting in Happy Chandler's bar in Colorado. They sat in one of the ancient wooden tables.

"I'm paying. Drink up," he had said. Then: "Why don't you take your coat off?"

"I'd only have to put it on again when we leave."

"We?"

"That's what you have in mind, ain't it?"

"I... I guess so."

"Don't you know?"

33

"It's what I have in mind." She remembered he had seemed so bashful, but then she was a business girl, and she told him so.

"I'm a business girl. Good hard business. I'm sociable for a price. Just understand that. Now, your place or mine."

She smiled to the bus window as the memory of the shock when she realized what Glen really was. It was in her room a few minutes after they had left the bar. She had had what must be called an apartment, certainly an inexpensive one, but nevertheless a three room apartment. There was always coffee for her guests, but she preferred the gin Glen had brought, and she brought out two glasses and a bottle of ginger ale. From the outset, she thought Glen had been overly interested in the red satin knee-length cocktail dress. But then, at the moment, she had passed it off as strictly an admiration for a really beautiful dress. Then he said: "Bet you even wear red undies."

She had simply stood up after kicking off her red high-heeled shoes and unzipped the back of the dress and let it fall to a circle around her ankles. She stood revealed in red satin brassiere and red satin panties. "Like 'em?"

"I love them." Again she had felt something more in the words than he was letting on. But the thought disappeared when he said, "I bet you've even got a red crotch." She had let the panties drift down on top of the dress. Glen had been right.

Then she walked into her bedroom to remove the brassiere and slip into a red satin

34

wraparound robe. When she came back into the living room, Glen had killed off his drink. She sank to the divan and motioned for him to join her, which he readily did. She took his hand and put it on the inside of her naked thigh. It was hot. Her body heat promised of more goodies to come. She moved his hand slowly up and down, back and forth. She leaned against the back of the divan. Her eyes closed in the ecstasy of the moment. A light whimpering came from between her closed lips, a sound which belied the enjoyment her body now possessed. Her hand moved his more rapidly. Then it was over as quickly as it had started. She let go of his hand, reached up and dragged his head down to hers. Her tongue darted in and out of his mouth. Her hot breath came out in deep gasps. Then his tongue was searching out every ripple of her hot mouth. The pain of their combined heat was only a pain of pure delight. She knew he wanted to run his tongue over every round inch of her body, and she wanted him to do it. She had wanted him on the bed, but the heat, the delightful pain of the heat could only make her squirm. His tongue found her breasts. One nipple then the other, back and forth with the suction of a windshield wiper in a heavy rainstorm. His tongue, his ever-pleasing hot tongue, found her navel, then the inside of her thighs. It was too much... this one really knew what he was doing. It was much too much... she wanted to cry out for release. He had put a fire to her a second time in almost as many minutes. There was no stopping the surge of joy which suddenly burst forth within her. Then they lay in each other's arms for a long moment. Glen had not even had a chance to take off his clothes, but it wasn't long before the young stud was ready again.

Red had slowly pulled away. "Not yet, lover... not yet again..." But she had locked her lips briefly to his. "I do have a bedroom, you know. Why don't you get your clothes off and we try the bed on for size?"

"Sure. Let me have one of your robes... I don't like parading around in the nude." That should have given her all the clue she needed, but it seemed, at the time, a logical request. But when she returned carrying a blue satin robe her eyes went wild at the sight of Glen standing there in a pink chemise and pink panties which he always wore under his male attire. She had put her hands on her hips, still holding the robe. "I should have known. The plucked eyebrows. Those long nails with the pearl polish. I should have guessed it."

She crossed to him and helped him slip into the robe; she even belted it to the left around his middle. "What do we do now? Make more lesbian love? I sure should have known. Nobody has a hot tongue like you got unless they're a little queer... oh, that hot tongue..." She convinced herself that no matter what he was, he was good.

"Do you want me to leave?"

"You're footing the bill."

"I'd do better if we weren't on such a business basis. Can't we be on more friendly terms?"

"Could be. When I get a little more drunk.

Maybe you'd like one of my nighties to go with that robe—or maybe my fox-trimmed negligee?" She grinned sardonically. "I can charge rent on wardrobe, you know."

"Damn it, drag the whole thing out," and he threw a hundred dollar bill on the floor in front of her.

Her eyes went wide as she picked up the bill. "A hundred bucks? This is ten times my price."

"I'm ten times better. I proved that a minute ago."

"Honey, for a hundred bucks you can be all the bother you want. You can be all the girl you want. I'll be the boy. I'll be the girl. Who the hell cares? For a hundred bucks you can wear anything I've got. I'll treat you any way you want." She got up and raced into the bedroom and was out in seconds with a blue satin nightgown. She helped him quickly out of the robe and slipped the straps of his chemise down under the garment circled in a soft cloud of pink around his ankles. There were only the pink panties left. Slowly, her hands went down his naked sides. They slipped into the top of his panties. She was slowly lowering them, and when they fell into the soft pink cloud already there, her arms locked around his waist. For a moment she rose up and her tongue flicked hotly over his boyish nipples. Then her knees seemed to sag, and her tongue made a straight line down his middle and to his manhood.

Glen wanted her, and he wanted her that way; she knew it from the moment she touched him. But he reached over and picked her up and kissed her long and hard. Then he took the nightgown from her hands and let it slip down over his head. He kissed her hotly again, their tongues meeting with all the power of the damned and the bedamned and when he took his mouth from hers again, he indicated the front of his nightgown. "Now," he said, so simply and softly. His meaning was all too clear and she loved the clarity of the meaning. Slowly, she let her hands drift down the sides of his lean body, over the satin material, and her knees slowly bent until they reached the floor. She lifted the hem of the blue satin nightgown and her eyes were wide at what she saw. Then she let the hem of the nightgown come down over her own head. Glen's hands held her head in place and she knew he had as wide a rapture of the moment as she herself had.

She had done it that way with many men over the years, but there had never been anyone she more enjoyed it with. She had loathed the experience most of the time, when she wasn't too drunk. But with Glen it wasn't like the other. With Glen it was love. She had known it from their first contact. So what if he liked to wear girls' clothes? The clothes was where he stopped being a girl. The rest was all male, no matter how he did it. And later, in the bedroom, when they were in a more conventional position and her desires had again mounted she had moaned: "Sweet love, sweet love... oh my boy, my girl, my sweet love. Take me. Take me as you want me..."

Over and over on the long bus ride she thought of her red sweater on the glorious body of Glenda... her very best one... the one he wore when he raced out of town two jumps ahead of the law. She wanted right then to call him back and once more feel his strong manhood through the soft materials of her own clothing. But more so, she remembered the love of Glenda's body beside her in bed. They had never been nude together. Glen would have no other than Glenda make their sex life. And Glenda had always insisted both have some sort of feminity on their bodies. Her thoughts drifted to the first time they had been together, and to Glenda that first morning, wearing the blue satin nightie and the red mohair bed-jacket. She had made breakfast, then they had gone back to bed for another session, a session only Glenda could perform. Later, when she had buried her head deep into the fur of Glenda's mohair bedjacket, she told the boy/girl how she had been in jail and what she had to do for the matrons in order to get along. It was the first time she had been subjected to lesbianism. But she had to live. And sooner or later she knew she would get out of jail and she wanted her face to be as pretty when she came out as when she had gone in.

"It must have been lousy for you." Glenda had been so comforting, so very understanding. How could anyone not love such a guy?

"Lousy! That's a little enough word for it. Work the fields or the mill all day then entertain the matrons all night. Maybe now you can understand a little of what I felt last night when I first saw you, like that, in drag. Sure! For

39

the hundred I guessed I could stand anything. Then a strange thing happened. Your tenderness to me. Clinging to your soft, yet commanding body. Your hands so tightly around my head under your nightgown. Something came over me that changed my every feeling toward you. I knew then I wanted you with all my senses. Hour after hour last night, I longed for just one more time. To have you inside of me just one more time. I didn't want the night to ever end. I never wanted you to leave. I've had people of your strange desires before, I cannot deny it—even worse—but not with the talent for pure love you possess." Then she rolled him over on top of her and all she could moan was: "Jazz me, sweet love... oh hurry... jazz me... for God's sake hurry... jazz... jazzzzz..." It had rained all that night and day too.

The pictures her mind projected blurred against the rain-drenched bus windows, but were not so blurred as to erase the exacting pictures from her mind. Glen had been so handsome, and Glenda so beautiful. She smiled at the rememberance of loving both in bed... both in their own special way. Rose had never been had until she met Glen/Glenda... then she *had* been had... there would never be anyone else. All experience wrapped up in one human being! It seemed impossible, and only a short time before, she might have believed it to be so. But the two persons in one body had proved to her a difference.

New York stretched out in all its glory before her. It was night, and it seemed the rain had followed her across the entire country. Her finances were going to be in miserable shape very soon, but it was too late to look up Glen's friend Barbara, and she was tired—much too tired to sit up all night on the hard bus terminal benches. It was apparent she would have to get a room for the night and that room turned out to be in a cheap, second-rate fleabag of a hotel, very close to the bus station. The cold, drenching rain forced her to no second decision—besides, Rose Graves was no stranger to cheap hotels and cheap rooming houses. She could handle herself.

But Rose found a way of not paying for her room that night. Her benefactor, in the form of a stop-over truck driver, paid for the room plus an extra five bucks for her attributes. The truck driver had not been a pleasant man, nor had he been gentle in his demand. Rose had liked her men rough, but she had been tired. On his third time around he demanded and got lip stimulation, but with one attraction he hadn't bargained for. She bit down hard—a pain he wouldn't soon forget. The man, when he got over the first shock, slapped her a resounding blow, put on his pants and shirt, then left the room. Rose had calmly gotten off the bed with her red nylon nightgown trailing her, locked the door, not that it would do much good, then immediately fell back into the bed, and within seconds she was deep in exhausted, restless sleep.

Barbara Benton hadn't been hard to find. She was still at the same address Glen had given for her. Rose first showed her Glen's note, then told her new acquaintance the story of their meeting, and of Mac and Ernie. Barbara had listened intently. Rose smoothed the red blouse and red cardigan down over the top of her red skirt as she finished.

"You poor kid," soothed Barbara.

"I'm alright now."

Barbara picked up a pack of cigarettes and a silver lighter from a marble table. Barbara had an elaborate layout. "Cigarette?"

"Yes, thank you," and she took one.

The brunette lit the cigarette for Rose. "Was Glen well when you left him?"

"Yes!" Rose spoke through the grey smoke then let a grin cross her face. "As well as could be expected with two cops on his tail."

Barbara lit her own cigarette and replaced both the package and lighter on the marble table before she spoke again. When she did speak, it was with some deep, hidden meaning. Rose caught the worded inflection, but believed it to be a slight bit of jealousy, only natural when it was apparent both had investigated Glen's entire body under the softness of a set of sheets.

"Did he say where he was going?"

"Yes."

Barbara forced a smile as she turned back to face Rose. "Where was it?" Then quickly. "I still have one of Glenda's mink jackets. I know he'd like to have it and I'd like to return it to him."

"I... I can't. Not just now anyway." Rose lowered her head. "It was a promise. He asked me to tell no one. Not even you. I'm sorry, so very sorry, Barbara."

Barbara laughed. "I don't blame you, honey. I'd have done the same for him. Look, where are you staying?"

"No place. Last night I stayed at a fleabag hotel. But all the lice aren't in the mattresses."

"Yeah, I know. Some are on top of it. Your bags there?"

"My suitcase is in a locker at the bus station."

"Good. Go pick it up. You're going to stay here with me until you get acclimatized."

"But I don't want to put you out any."

"Look at the place. Big as a temple. There's plenty of room. Besides, I won't take no for an answer. Glen would want me to do it this way. Need some money?"

"Oh, no... no thanks." She paused. "Are you sure?"

"I'm sure. Now, get going. Maybe I'll have us lined up for a date tonight by the time you come back." Barbara held her broad grin.

Rose took a cab back downtown. After all, she could afford the extra five dollars—and it didn't look like she would have to pay any rent for a while. She'd even ask the taxi driver to wait while she went to the locker, picked up her lone suitcase and have him drive her back uptown to Barbara's. And she did just that.

Rose carried her own suitcase to Barbara's apartment. She pushed open the door. Four pug-uglies were waiting for her. One of them, a big man with a scar on his cheek, pulled a gun from his belt. "Know what this is?"

Rose looked into each of their stern faces, then to the unconcerned features of Barbara, who wore a set of gold satin lounging pajamas and held a tall whiskey in her hand. She spoke without looking to Rose. "It's the breaks of the game, honey."

"She said it right, honey. It's the breaks of the game." The man with the scar got up out of his chair and slapped Rose a stinging blow across her face, a blow that caused her to drop the suitcase, which split open, spilling its meagre contents on the floor. "Now we're going for a little ride. And if you get outta' line that slap is only the beginning. My gun will slap you harder, and sometimes it makes bad cuts." Scarface turned to Barbara. He indicated the ruptured suitcase and the articles spewn on the floor. "Burn that crap when we leave."

COMPOSITE REPORT #1—ROSE 'RED' GRAVES

Rose could hold her breath no longer—a great gasp of air bubbles exploded from her lungs. The bubbles drifted up through the black, cold water. Her eyes opened to watch them for one last hypnotic moment and her mind gasped for one last thought. It was when the skinny, hawk-nosed creep stripped off her red sweater, skirt and undies, then carefully put them in a luggage case, and as she was revealed to their

44

eyes completely naked, one of the pug-uglies touched the hair of her crotch and said: "Look there! She really is a redhead!"

"Glen... Glenda... forgive me..."

Then the water of the Hudson filled her lungs and the tranquility of oblivion became overpowering...

CHAPTER FIVE

WARDEN'S NOTE

With the cab driver's report (L.A. Police Report #795) of delivering the Killer to the Strader Motel on the Sunset Strip, it was decided the establishment should be investigated. Subsequently, enough evidence was uncovered to arrest the employees for the charges of bookmaking and procuring. A bellboy, looking for an easy way out, told that he had been paid by persons unknown in the East to watch the Killer.

L.A. POLICE REPORT #9113—FRED HENT— BELLBOY—STRADER MOTEL

At the motel on the Sunset Strip, the Killer put his well-traveled but unobtrusive luggage on a well-made bed. After a time he opened it. From underneath a carefully laundered bunch of shirts and an extra suit, the hawk-nosed Killer produced a German Luger. He checked the loads, then put it on the bed, very near the pillow.

Without investigating the remainder of the articles in the bag, he reached for, and opened, one of the smaller ones and his eyes gleamed with a strange desire as he smoothed out the red skirt, the red sweater, the red panties, brassiere and a slip.

He realized then he had to get a pair of red shoes. The ones the whore had on were three sizes too small for him, so they had gone to the bottom of the river with her.

The red outfit—her red outfit. It could hasten all his plans. He didn't like Hollywood. He didn't like anything about it: the complete hassle to get out of the airport area; the stupid, even crazy drivers on the freeways; the accidents he witnessed even in his short duration on them. At least on the tollways in New York, the people had to stop their cars every so often to pay the toll fees. It kept them in line, kept their speed down. But that Sepulveda Freeway which eventually led to the Hollywood Freeway—that was too much! The cab driver wasn't of any help. But he knew he had a fare, a mark, and he wanted to deliver that fare as soon as possible, get his money—plus tip—and then be on his way again for another. Even at that, and the Killer knew it, the cabbie had followed his natural instincts—the law of the jungle—screw or get screwed. Just the way they did it in New York. I got myself a sucker, let's take the long way round.

The cabbie turned off on the Vine Street exit of the freeway; the Killer saw the move. Then the cab lurched as the driver turned right off of Vine on Sunset, then he doubled back to the Strader Motel on the Sunset Strip. It was an extra two bucks in the driver's pocket, and his tip had been an extra two bucks.

The Killer looked down at the red female attire on the bed. Suddenly the urge came over

47

him. As of that moment he hadn't put those garments on his body, but now, the overwhelming urge was a torment to him in mind and tingling body. Overwhelming! The Killer nearly tore off his clothing then, much more slowly, hawk-nose put on each of the red garments. Slowly... so slowly... the panties... the adjustment of the brassiere... the slip, so slowly drifting down over his head... the skirt, fastened tightly around the red nylon slip, then the soft wool of the sweater. The Killer—Pauline—could stand it no longer. She raced to the bathroom where she did what she had to do for her climax.

It had been the first time Pauline had—*had*—to climax, to do it for herself, without waiting for her wig and since before she had owned one.

There had to be something in the red outfit she had not expected. Perhaps the lingering perfume. Perhaps the smell of an underwater element. But Pauline broke her resistance with an upraised red skirt and a spreading of the red panty-leg, his hand working feverishly for his own selfish climax. The girl on the bottom of the Hudson River waiting for the time the fish would clean her bones of flesh and guts... that girl no longer existed. She was gone.

Pauline cleaned herself off, looked into the bathroom mirror, then turned to flush the toilet.

It had been a situation of the moment. The Syndicate was watching, waiting. Paul, the Killer, had to guard his fondest desires until his job was finished.

He took off the red sweater, skirt, panties, brassiere and slip and put them all over a chair.

Tomorrow would be soon enough.

If Glen had liked the broad in red, then Glen would find another in red... blood red.

CHAPTER SIX

GLEN MARKER'S CONFESSION—TAPE

I turned my road-stained convertible onto the Hollywood Freeway as I criss-crossed off the San Bernardino Freeway. A long time before, early that morning just outside of Las Vegas, Nevada, Glenda had shed her white angora sweater and the blue velvet skirt for my brown suit, white shirt and brown tie.

The Los Angeles green-gray smog with its light rotten-egg smell greeted my sense of smell just after I had left San Bernardino, and by the time I reached Pomona it had further become an eye-stinging mess. A sudden spring heat-wave mixed with the fact of practically no rain and not the slightest breeze, kept the lung-choking smog in thick clouds.

It was as I took a handkerchief from my pocket to wipe the stinging tears from my eyes the slight accident occurred. Two cars ahead, someone had, for one reason or another, jammed on their brakes. Each in turn, behind the offending cars, tore up the rear of the other, suffering front grille-work damage themselves. I, still with handkerchief in hand, but with the training of immediate decisions, flipped my steering wheel to the right, at the same time jamming on my own brakes. With screeching, smoking tires, my car finally came to a jarring halt. I had saved

50

my front end, but at the expense of my own rear. Not much damage, but damage all the same.

Almost at the instant of collision, four Los Angeles motorcycle policemen raced into the scene. Immediately they set up red flares. I started to get out of the injured convertible, but a nearby guarding policeman angrily snapped a straight arm to me and just as angrily snapped his words. "Keep in your car!"

I was in strange territory. I was not about to argue the situation. I got back in my car and closed the door, then waited.

I couldn't help but marvel at the efficiency of the Los Angeles Police Department in their appointed duties. Within minutes, the cars were moved off to the shoulder of the freeway where a sign boldly proclaimed: Emergency Parking Only.

None of the cars in the accident were so damaged as to hinder their motors from turning over, and at least getting them off to the side of the freeway, where on seeing the others getting out of their cars, I followed suit.

The girl came out of the car behind, also a convertible but a late model Cadillac, white, with all the extras. I noticed immediately and approved of the things she wore. Pink capris, pink high- heeled slippers and a long-sleeved, black nylon blouse. Her solid blue-black hair seemed almost lost at the silky ends as it drifted over the black blouse at her shoulders. She moved slowly toward me as I in turn moved back toward her.

"Sorry I got in your way," I grinned.

The extremely beautiful, black-haired girl

smiled broadly. "You certainly tried hard enough to keep out of my way!" She stretched out her hand. "I'm Cynthia Harland."

I figured, the way she said it, her name was supposed to mean something, but I just smiled pleasantly and took her hand lightly in my own. "I'm Glen Marker."

"Pretty good pile-up, I'd say." She was smiling again.

"Does this happen often?" I let my hand sweep the area of incident.

"Every day. Sometimes three, four, ten times a day. And night! There are a lot of freeways around here. Millions of automobiles, trucks, cycles. You ever ride cycles, Mr. Marker?"

"Oh, I've been on them, but I'm not what you might call an enthusiast."

"Real excitement." Her eyes closed momentarily as if she had gone off into dreamland. Then when she opened them again, her words were ones of information. "A lot of actors and actresses around Hollywood ride them these days. Except when they are on a picture. Most of the producers have clauses in their contracts forbidding it during the shooting schedule."

"I can well understand why," I replied, then added. "Are you an actress?"

"I... I work at it. Your license plate," she laughed while pointing to the damaged identification tag. "What's left of it that is, tells me you're from Colorado. Did you come to be in movies?"

"I hadn't thought of it one way or the other."

"You're handsome enough for the movies!"

For the first time in a great many years, I

nearly blushed. "Thank you," I stammered.

"I didn't mean that as a passing compliment. It's a simple fact."

"I've always heard it takes a lot more than looks to be an actor: good, bad or indifferent." I tried to match her growing grin.

The motorcycle policeman who had ordered me back into my car earlier came up to us. "Now," he started, then recognized my face. "You were the character trying to play footsies on the freeway out there."

"The accident... I was..."

The officer cut me off abruptly. He pointed that same straight arm back to the freeway where cars of every size, make, description and length traveled at tremendous speeds. "You see that out there."

It was not a question. "Hundreds of those vee-hickles cross that same spot every few seconds, day and night."

"Sorry officer," I said simply.

"Sorry? You should be! You should be thoughtful and damned thankful you're still alive. Get out of a car out there and Las Vegas wouldn't give odds. I should give you a citation, but since you're from Colorado you don't know the law here. When you're in a collision on any freeway, you stay in your vee-hickle until help arrives and tells you to get out. And that won't be ever in the middle of the freeway."

An ambulance arriving for an injured party in the front car caused a momentary interruption in the motorcycle officer's tirade. He stepped out from behind the cars to look ahead to the action. The black-haired girl took me lightly by the arm.

"Don't make him angry," she whispered close to my ear.

"I'm trying not to!"

"They're nice guys, most of these cops around here—unless you give them some lip."

"I've noticed their size. I'm not interest in problems."

The policeman came back to face us, and this time he had his pad open. "May I see both of your driver's licenses?"

The girl and I produced our driver's licenses and the officer took down the girl's information first, then handed her license back to her. Finally he turned to me. He took up the license and wrote down that information also. It seemed like an eternity to me as the pencil scratched on the pad. Then he looked up from the license, then to the car and back to my eyes. "Your driver's license reads New York issuance... and your car reads Colorado."

I started to reach swiftly toward my left hip pocket, but froze as the cop reached for, and had his pistol drawn in an instant.

The black-haired girl stepped quickly between us. "Now, boys," she said. "It's only a traffic situation."

"I was only going for my wallet again."

"You'd better not have a gun, buster." He kept his pistol on me as he moved forward.

"Why in hell should I need a gun?"

The cop stopped within a few feet of me. "What's in the wallet?"

"My bill of sale for the car—the pink slip—and my registration is on the steering wheel."

54

"Let's see the wallet. Make it a slow move." A second officer stepped in curiously as the first spoke.

I was slow in my move. I took the wallet from my pocket and extracted the bill of sale and the pink slip. The officer looked at it, made a note, then returned them both to me. "You better learn not to make sudden moves when an officer is questioning you." After that, he turned and left us to go on about further business at the other end.

The black-haired beauty moved in close to me again. "I'm Cynthia Harland!"

I was putting the wallet back into my pocket as she had spoken. "You told me that before," I said.

She was silent for another long moment. "The cops... they're just doing a job... the job they're paid for!"

"Somewhere I've heard that before." My voice wasn't so condescending.

Cynthia led me to a rise on the side of the freeway where new grass and plants were abundant. We sank, at her light direction, to a reclining position. "A lot of cops have been killed in a move like you just made back there."

"Reaching for my wallet?"

"You were reaching for your wallet." She paused again pointedly. "How could the cop really know? A fast move like that generally means a gun. Lucky the cop wasn't trigger-happy. It's happened, you know."

I sat up startled.

"There have been a lot of cops falling into the roadway, gunned down by somebody to

55

whom the cop was only going to give a ticket."

"Is that a fact?"

"You'll be reading about it if you stay around Los Angeles very long. That's fact."

"Some creeps will do anything to get their name in the papers." I leaned back on the grass beside the beautiful girl again. "What happens now, Miss Cynthia Harland—or is it Mrs?"

"Miss," she said softly. "They'll finish up pretty quick, then we'll be on our way. First, the cops will determine who is at fault—well, find out what insurance company will pay off—then we can take to the road again and see if we can find another accident on the way to happen."

"Can I see you again?" I had looked at her a long time before I decided to voice my desires.

The beautiful black-haired girl laughed lightly, knowingly. She sat up and fluffed her hair over her shoulders. She indicated the white Cadillac convertible just below us. "You see that?"

"Who could help but see it."

"That's from my sugar daddy."

I winked. "I didn't think you were old enough to afford it yourself." It was not meant as an insult.

"Fresh!" She plonked down on the grass again. "Actresses make enough money for such things... or didn't you know?"

"I know."

She gave a sly little pout. "I could be an actress."

"Are you?"

"No."

"As beautiful as you are?"

She turned her lovely face slightly toward me. She made a suggestive thing with her beautiful red lips. "You say the nicest things, Mr. Marker. You should be my agent."

"In that case, forget the Mr. Marker and call me Glen."

"Glen." She rolled the word, the name over in her mouth as if she were tasting it. And from the sexy look which suddenly came to her eyes, she liked what she was tasting. "I like it!"

"My name?"

"Your name. Glen..." She closed her eyes and pressed her lips as if in a kiss. "I like it."

"I don't suppose you live with your sugar daddy?"

"He sees me twice a week."

" That still leaves five days."

"I never know what days he will be in town."

"Haven't you got a back door?"

"Two of them."

We both laughed. "When?" I asked, pushing my advantage.

"I didn't say you could!"

"At least your phone number!"

"I never give it out..." she looked off to the police officers who were writing down requested information, "... except," she continued. "If the police asked me for it. And my address, I couldn't help it if someone were to overhear, now could I?"

I was not surprised.

CHAPTER SEVEN

L.A. POLICE REPORT #9113—FRED HENT— BELL BOY

The Killer, dressed in gray trousers and a Hawaiian-type sports shirt, on his first day in Hollywood, did much as any tourist might. He went sightseeing. But he didn't join any guided tours. He wanted to know Hollywood Boulevard and the area of Sunset Boulevard known as the Sunset Strip. It was in those two well-advertised sections Glen would be found if he was to be found at all.

He knew Glen liked the bright lights where the action was. He also knew Glen would be searching out the gay bars where his own kind frequented. It would be pleasant work all the way for the Killer because he also appreciated the gay life just as much as Glen ever could. But above all, he liked to kill.

The Syndicate couldn't have picked a better assassin in that respect, because the Killer did his job with the coldness and with the calculation of a striking cobra. And he was just as deadly.

WARDEN'S NOTE

Gathering information on Paul Hefner's youth came more easily than I had anticipated. It seemed little of his life, then, was a secret; almost as if someday he wanted to tell his story. He kept a diary right up until the time he had left New York for Los Angeles, and the diary was discovered in a locked compartment of his liquor cabinet in his apartment.

N. Y. POLICE FILE #398—PAUL 'PAULINE' HEFNER—CONDENSED DIARY

There had to be something in life he could do well. Ever since he was a small child he'd been the ugly duckling who did everything wrong, was laughed at by the girls, even as far back as kindergarten. Of course, little did he know it at the time, but a pattern of deep-seated hatred was forming rapidly in his character which would last throughout his life.

In his very early teens he had raped and killed three high school girls, classmates of his, and he had never been caught. He found then how much he enjoyed killing—killing anyone or anything.

And it was in those three rape-murders that another pattern took shape in his mind. Unique, he thought.

With the first he simply cut her dress and undies from her body and raped the girl, both of them naked. When he was finished, the girl passed out and he thought she was dead, but he put his knife four times into her heart. Then she was dead for sure.

The second one he caught in a schoolyard, beyond the baseball field. He had watched her and a boy he knew from the basketball team.

They had petted and tongued and felt each other until the Killer thought he'd go mad in anticipation. But that was as far as the boy and the girl went. Finally, the basketball player went off his way and the girl started off in her direction. The Killer held her mouth and nose until she passed out, then he tore off her panties and raped her while she was fully dressed, but he was stark-naked. The chill of the late summer air had meant nothing to him as he waited and watched. The heat of his pent-up emotions permitted no chill to pierce his body. However, as he raped this unconscious girl, something did pierce his skin. It was a feeling, a strange sensation which he paused in his action to analyse. Then he knew what it was. The girl wore a fuzzy, brushed wool sweater which was buttoned up the front. It seemed to move against his skin with a sexual stimulation he had never experienced before. To be sure, very sure, he let his hands slowly caress the softness of the garment at the point where her breasts stretched the wool so invitingly. Then he was sure. The electricity of the sensation shot through to his groin. He could hardly contain himself as his nervous, shaking hands unbuttoned the fur-like sweater and took it from her body. Just as shakily he put it slowly onto his own body and the ecstasy of the moment as he buttoned it up caught a craving within him so intense he nearly exploded before he could get back with the girl and complete his climax the way he always had before. She died with her throat cut, but it was the start of a *collection* for the Killer.

When Rita Styles died, in a like manner, her clothing added to that *collection*. After he had undressed her unconscious body, he stripped, then dressed from the skin out in her things. Her panties, still warm with the girl's body heat, started him off to even more powerful craving desires. He took the girl with such force that both the girl's legs were broken at the knees. And brazenly he had carried his own pants and shirt while he wore her clothing, blood spattered as they were, all the way home. He had lived, during those late teen years, in a room over the garage of his mother's home. There he had all the privacy he needed and wanted. Even when his room started to take on the ruffles and pink of femininity, his mother approved. There was little he did that she didn't approve. She had given him life and love, but very little in looks, and she tried desperately, at every chance, to make it up to him. Her first inkling that the infant would be thoroughly lacking in the looks department came when she saw no change in the face at a time the baby wrinkles and redness should have gone. But the condition didn't go. The wrinkles and creases persisted up until the time the kid's nose started into its prominence. A hawk-like nose which would bring the boy many harrowing days and nights with other children. His mother continually, to the day she died, blamed herself for her own indiscretions. She had never married. The man who fathered the boy took her when they were both drunk on cheap gin in the back seat of an automobile. And when the man had finished his own lust, he slammed the woman in her stomach with his fist then kicked her out of the car and drove off. Paul had been born of an affair which didn't even have love connected with it.

As it usually happened on such events, his mother arrived at his garage-top room unexpectedly. She was quite amazed to see her son dressed in pink capris, a pink nylon blouse which was well-decorated with frills and pink sandals, but she was not sent into shock. More so, she was confused, but not offended.

The young killer studied her appraising glance, then he moved with unsure femininity to sit in a large easy chair. "You don't like what you see, Mother?"

The woman took a long time in answering. She first went into his refrigerator and poured a glass of cold tea, a beverage which the young Paul was seldom without. Then she walked back to a chair across from him and sat down. Again, quietly, she took a few sips. After that, she looked across the rim of the glass. "It is Pauline, isn't it?"

He matched her gaze. "I hadn't thought much about a name. Before, that is. Paul... Pauline..." He let his eyes rest on a pack of cigarettes and a silver lighter. "I think I'll give up smoking." But he took a cigarette from the pack and lit it, then let the light gray smoke drift up around his head. "My hair will have to be longer... I'd rather it be that way than attempt a wig."

"You've made up your mind?"

"Some time ago..."

The woman sighed, but it was not an air-expounding sigh, more so a sigh of simple acceptance. "What about school?"

"I've decided to quit school!"

"Then what?"

Pauline, and it was Pauline, threw herself out of the chair to prance back and forth across the small confines of the room, hips swinging, limp wrists activating themselves.

"Who cares then? There will always be something I can do… maybe a secretary… yes, that's it… I'll be a secretary…"

"In drag?"

The Killer glanced sharply to his mother. "Where'd you learn that word?" There was a deep-set anger in his tone.

"Your father has been gone a long time!"

"I've never had a father per se. Where did you learn that word?"

His mother let her eyes flick a few times as she tried to find suitable words. "As I started to say. The man who was your father has been gone a long time." She blinked again, then let her eyes fall. "There are certain things a woman needs."

"Sex!" Paul stamped his foot in the manner of a spoiled little girl who hasn't gotten her way. "Say it, Mother—sex! Isn't that what a woman always seems to need?"

She looked up with the sad eyes of a hound dog. "There is a crowd I have associated with who are in tune with such things. Such people who feel as you do!"

Pauline threw up her hands. "Such people who feel as I do! How can they feel as I do and refer to all this," he indicated the female attire he was wearing, as drag? It isn't done! I am not a drag. I am a true woman. Just as true as I can be, as long as the stupidity of what is called manhood remains connected to me." He threw himself into the flowered chair, and he cried. "I am a girl. I am! I am! I am!" The frustration came pouring out in a rush of nearly lost words.

His mother indecisively waited a long time before she walked across to him and seated herself on the chair beside him where she cuddled his head in her arms. As his tears flowed freely she let her hand stroke his forehead. "Of course you are," she cooed. "Of course you are. You're my baby Pauline... my little girl... my little girl Pauline."

And the Killer stalked the Sunset Strip. His beady, snake-like eyes never missed a face or a move. In one quick glance around he knew every corner in any establishment he drifted into. His decisive mind knew immediately to eliminate the square joints. They were, he was sure, not in value with Glen's way of thinking. The gay bars were his prey, and in each, the Killer was looked upon with ever-growing suspicions. There came almost hostility to the eyes of the gay boys and girls whom he came in contact with: a distrust brought on by their own years of frustration. There are none, as the Killer knew well, who would trust him immediately, and he figured it would be the same with him.

Whom could he trust? In the same fact, who in even the square world of the outsider, could be trusted?

The Killer had to smile in his own knowledge, and his eyes watched the ones who were dressed like girls but he knew to be boys, and the butch bull dykes in their old work trousers and grey work-shirts... and those others who would like to be dressed as one or the other, but lacked the guts to make the attempt except in the confines of their own rooms, where they could dress up, admire themselves in a full-length mirror and do what they had to for their own self-gratification.

A long time before, when Pauline's mother caressed his forehead while he cried the tears of frustration she had said: "Sexual gratification comes only from the tune one plays within themselves."

He found that to be fact over the long years he continued to live, and find solace in himself and in the criminal acts he finally was called upon to perform.

In the beginning, when Pauline met Harvey, it was only for an experience that he took him on. There had been a night, about the time he'd turned twenty, that he went to a bar and met Harvey. A nice-looking young fellow who had simply said 'Hello', and a drink for each came into being. Then a walk in the park where the young man suggested they sit down, which they did for a short time. The young man then suddenly leaned over and kissed Paul, and Paul wanted the young man, but didn't want it the way he was dressed.

For a goodly time, Paul had been the girl, and to have at it with a man, Paul had to be the girl, or at least retain the illusion that he was a girl. He couldn't even fathom having any kind of sex in the nude—it was repulsive to him—except he felt his partner, the male counterpart should be naked. But he, Pauline, must hide the horrors of his own masculinity which resided between his legs. The horror of masculinity he'd rather do without, but the kind of masculinity Pauline appreciated in another.

Harvey became the counterpart in their frequent love affairs, and for a while Pauline was happy and content without any thoughts of rape and murder which had previously so dominated his waking hours. All was serene rapture, a pleasant experience. They became as one, Pauline the girl and Harvey the boy, like any other set of young lovers. The identity of Paul was rapidly lost to Pauline; she no longer wore male attire at all; it was the way she and Harvey wanted and enjoyed it. Their sex life was powerful—ruggedly violent, yet a tremendous inspiration of mind and body.

They decided to get married during one of their Sunday sessions. Legally married. Reno was only an overnight trip from the small Northern town, and they quickly decided Reno would be the quickest and safest solution to their problems.

Her mother was immediately receptive to the idea, in fact overjoyed at the prospect. She had long since, and had diligently worked toward it, accepted Pauline and all Pauline stood for.

"We'd like you to go with us, Mother." stated Pauline as she slipped into her long, white wedding dress and adjusted the veil and train of lace back over her long hair. She then let her hands slip lazily along the slinky lines of the satin gown. "Do you like it, Mother?"

"It's beautiful, darling."

"Do you think Harvey will like it?"

"Harvey will like anything you wear!"

"Dear Harvey. Will you, Mother? Come

with us?"

The woman let her eyes rove over the dress. She took up a thin seam just over the hip-line. Measuringly she said. "I can take a slight tuck in there, it will give your hip-line a bit more roundness." She stood back in deep thought. "Yes, I think that will do it rather nicely." Then the tears of resignation welled in her eyes. "Do you and Harvey really want me with you?"

Pauline swished the skirts of her white satin wedding dress around her legs as she looked deep, seriously, into her mother's eyes. "Any girl wants her mother at hand when she gets married." Pauline let the brightness of her glow penetrate through to her mother, and her mother walked across to look through the second-storey window. She gazed for a long time out over the browns and yellows of Fall. She was happy for her self-made daughter, but she couldn't seem to put the emotion into actual force. As hard as she tried for a true feeling, it only came out a superficial expression. There seemed to be an inevitable disaster lurking in the late afternoon shadows. There was no putting her finger directly on the cause, but it was there as sure as night followed day.

"Do you think the hem should be a bit longer, Mother?" The Killer's high-pitched voice brought the woman back to reality.

"Oh no, dear," she replied as she turned from the window. "Except for that little tuck, the gown is perfect just as it is."

Pauline scowled at her reflection in the mirror. "Such a lovely body in this dress. Now all I need is a new face." It was an extremely serious observation.

The mother put her arm around the satin-covered shoulders. "Beauty is only skin deep."

"Oh, that old routine. That idea went out with high-button shoes. You might just as well add: beauty is only in the eye of the beholder. Come on, Mother. Be your age. You've been around. You know what they used to call me at school? Hose-nose Gertie, that's what." The Killer let a hand run lightly over the protruding object. "Some day I'll have enough money to see what a doctor can do." Then, absently, Pauline's hand dropped down to where the rubber falsies underneath made a well-rounded appearance on the front of the dress. "And about making these real."

"If they were mine to give, you could have mine."

The Killer took his mother's hand almost tenderly. "I know you would, Mother."

Harvey drove the car with his bride-to-be, wearing a pink traveling suit, in the front seat beside him, while his mother-in-law to be, wearing an identical pink traveling suit, occupied the rear seat... and when the front tire blew and they hit the highway marker, the older woman seemed to fly over the front seat where her forehead crashed in against the windshield. She died instantly. Harvey hung between life and death for days, but by the time Paul had been released from the hospital, he had died.

Paul was not held for his masquerade, but he was questioned for a long time, then when no charges were filed, he was released but advised to leave the state. He did swiftly as he was told; there were too many things in his past which might be revealed through accidental conversations during questioning. The first time over, he wasn't about to be picked up a second time.

He took the bodies of his mother and his friend back to the small town where he buried them side by side. Of course, they had been with an undertaker near the scene of the accident for more than a month, but he asked for and got transportation, to make the move.

Whereby, thereafter, the Killer's old haunts steadily took over his mind again, but he killed only once more for his own pleasures: a hapless girl he had seen in the park who happened to be wearing an exceptionally beautiful, frilly white blouse which excited him to occult proportions. The girl died soundlessly, but Pauline gained a new article for his *collection*.

After that he turned his full talents to murder for pay. It had not been difficult for him to make a connection. A trip to New York City. A few purchases of narcotics on Harlem back streets. A few feigned non-payments of narcotic purchases and he was connected. The rest was easy!

But even as he gained confidence in the Syndicate there was always Glen Marker... the never-ending stories of the fabulous Glenda... the talented Glenda... The deadly Glenda.

Until Glenda fell out of grace with the Syndicate and Glen/Glenda was marked for immediate assassination. A job which fell to Paul/ Pauline. It was to be an execution which would make Pauline the leader in the field of execution.

And his eyes fought the coming darkness of

the Sunset Strip and the sudden dazzling lights, but he would continue, and he would learn as he moved. He would know the establishments. And sooner or later he would find his score.

CHAPTER EIGHT

GLEN MARKER'S CONFESSION—TAPE

I elected to remain in my hotel room for the first couple of days. Not a very interesting room in a sleazy hotel on Hollywood Boulevard near Vermont Avenue, but a room all the same. There had been many times during those long hours I couldn't help but feel the Syndicate was breathing down my back; the Syndicate I had served so faithfully in the past. However, that's all it was— a feeling, not a fact I could be sure of. I knew I'd have to classify myself as some kind of an idiot if I at least didn't give the thoughts the possibility of reality. I was not one to overlook any possibility which had only presented itself to the light of day, but also to those which tried to remain in the recesses of my mind.

The hours in my hotel room became heavy on my hands. I began to pace the floor, something I'd never done before in my life. For the first few days I had watched a cheap twelve-inch television set provided by the owners, and the shows, the variety of shows—nothing! I wished they would show an old Buck Jones or Jack Hoxie movie which I'd seen so many of during my youth at the Saturday matinees. There was action as action should be played, full and round.

I waited until a bellboy delivered the sandwiches I had ordered, then slipped into a blue

71

nylon nightgown and stretched out on the bed again. But sleep wouldn't come and I lay gazing at the gray ceiling. I knew it was simple boredom which kept my normal faculties from working, and the only cure for that was to get out of the room and do something: a change of pace and scenery.

Of course I realized enough to know I shouldn't attack the streets in female attire until I found the lay of the land. Not that I should be frightened of such an adventure. After all I had lived as a girl too long and in too many places to let something like that bother me. But for the time being I would progress slowly.

Then I got up and reluctantly removed the nightgown, slipped into a clean set of pink panties, dressed in my deep brown suit and went out onto Hollywood Boulevard where I hailed a taxi which took me to Upper Hollywood Boulevard. Since I had never seen the street before, I felt much like any other rubber-necking tourist, but the longer I walked, the more I realized there was little to really see on the famous Boulevard. A few brightly-lighted stores, a few cocktail bars and the names of movie personalities embedded in bronze stars in the sidewalk. "What the hell?" I mused, then turned my way along Vine Street until I found the Brown Derby where I entered into the cocktail lounge section.

Cynthia Harland was there, sitting in a rear booth with a well-dressed, gray-haired man—a man not at all bad-looking, but he was at least some thirty-odd years her senior. My first reaction was to reactivate our recent friendship. I started immediately across toward the couple, but as my approach took me to almost greeting distance, she caught my eye and I realized her hidden panic, then a slight movement to wave me off. I continued on to the men's room, with the recognition incomplete, where I stayed a prescribed amount of time, then I returned to the bar where I ordered a double Martini. Whiskey was my favorite drink, but in such a place as the Brown Derby, the inhabitants ran more toward the cocktail crowd. I would travel with the flock.

Cynthia caught my eye several times via the back-bar mirror and the glance was one of apology. I, of course, understood her position, and when it was safe I grinned my message across to her and she knew I understood.

But there was a burning deep inside of me which took me several moments to fully understand. Naturally I'd had most of the sensations any man found for any girl he'd like to make. However, this was deeper. It not only stirred my leg muscles, but added a twinge around my heart muscles and a fiery sensation in my face. I looked up to my image in the mirror and saw the anger I could read there. I was actually angry! But was it anger? Then I knew the feeling of jealousy... an emotion I had never experienced in my entire life. Jealousy in any form, of anything, wasn't part of my make-up. Yet there I sat in a famous Hollywood bar experiencing it for the first time toward a girl I hardly knew.

Her blue strapless cocktail dress and the white angora stole flipped me the moment I saw them, but there was more to my regular emotions this time. There was a blinding fury of her being with someone else when I wanted to be with her myself. I suddenly slammed my glass down and the bartender turned sharply to look at me. The reaction of sound and sight brought me to myself immediately. I forced a light smile to my lips and I muttered. "Sorry. It slipped."

The bartender brought a condescending grin to his face and moved to confront me with a bar towel which he used to mop up the small portion of the Martini which had splashed from the glass. "Happens to all of us. Want another?"

"Sure," I said as I reached in my pocket for some cash, which the bartender waved off.

"When you're ready to leave is time enough, sir," the bartender informed me, then mixed the drink and rang the amount up on a bar slip which he secured on the bar in front of me.

"Mighty friendly of you."

"Policy of the house, sir." He looked up and down the bar which was nearly empty since it was the lull between dinner-time and the shows letting out. "New in town?"

"Very."

"Tourist?"

"Not exactly. But I'm looking around."

"You've got the looks of an actor!"

I gazed into the mirror and laughed. "Not in any of the places I can see." Then my eyes caught sight of Cynthia and she was alone at the table. She caught my eye. But she was telling me she wanted to see me, but not then.

The bartender stepped away briefly to wait on a customer who came in and seated himself some distance up the bar, but in that brief moment I reached into my pocket and brought out my address book. I made contact, through the mirror, with Cynthia again and I tapped the address book. She nodded, then again quickly ducked her eyes as her escort returned from the direction of the men's room, and seated himself beside her once more.

I pocketed the address book, then picked up my drink as the bartender confronted me again. "Writer?"

I shook my head. "No, my friend. Frankly, I'm a hired killer."

The bartender went into peals of laughter which caused the manager, from across the room, to give him a sharp glance of reproach. The man stopped in the middle of a breath. "Okay. So I won't ask anymore."

"Then let me ask one."

"Shoot!"

"There's a girl sitting in the booth in the back." The bartender did not look up as I continued. "She's wearing a blue cocktail dress and a white angora stole. Do you know her?"

The man grinned. "Looks familiar?"

"Something like that."

"She should. Maybe she ain't a big star yet, but she will be one of these days, you just mark my words."

"Movies, huh? So that's where I saw her."

"She's done a lot of bit parts in the big flicks and then there's the television pictures and the commercials. She gets along. And one of these days she's gonna hit the top with a ring that will be heard like a symphony orchestra. Her name's Cynthia Harland. She comes in often."

"With the same cat she's with?"

"Nah... not always. Although when he's in town she's generally with him. Guess they got a thing going." He shrugged and refilled my glass from the remainder in a mixing jug. "Then who in hell knows in Hollywood? One minute they got something going... the next it's up the creek with a bunch of lawyers, cops and private detectives." A new thought hit the man. "Say, you a private eye?"

"Now," I replied seriously, "it's like I told you. I'm a hired killer." I let the grin replace my serious features.

"Yeah, I know... you told me. Only I can't laugh so loud anymore... the boss is watching. I think he got up on the wrong side of the bed this afternoon. He's been burping at the others all day. The guy's name is Ronald Dixon. He's broadcast manager for some television station up in San Francisco. Pretty big in the money bracket from what I understand."

"Probably has a wife!"

"Now you are making me think you're a private dick. Who knows? We here at the Brown Derby never pry into anybody's private life."

I frowned, but covered it with a swallow of my Martini, then as the bartender walked away I let my eyes drift up to the mirror again and saw Cynthia attempting to flick on her lighter which apparently would not ignite. Even when it did, the flame seemed to flicker immediately out. The man took the lighter from her and flicked it into flame, but again as she tried to light her cigarette the lighter went out immediately. Then my eyes were diverted as the maitre d' walked to her with a pack of matches, one of which he struck until her cigarette was glowing. Then he graciously put the matchbook on the table in front of her. She thanked him with her glowing smile, and he went back about his business of greeting another couple who called him to their table.

And further, as the man stood up later to pay the bill, he turned his back on Cynthia long enough for her to scribble something on the inside of the matchbook cover. Then they got up from the table. The man adjusted her angora stole around her shoulders and they started for the front door where she had to pass me. She dropped the matchbook at my feet.

I waited until the side parking lot door closed behind them, then I conveniently dropped my pack of cigarettes, which I had to retrieve, along with the matchbook, from the floor.

"Another Martini—killer?"

I snapped my hand to the man, an anger I hadn't felt since Mac and Ernie had accosted me so many days earlier, but I couldn't hold the anger in the face of the grinning bartender. After all, the killer bit had been propogated by my own wit. "Sure, why not?" I replied.

Still smiling, the bartender turned away and I took a cigarette from my pack and lit it with one of the matches from her book. The flame added to enhance my vision of the words scrawled on the inside of the packet. "Call me soon. Tomorrow at noon."

CHAPTER NINE

WARDEN'S NOTE

Cynthia Harland hadn't been attuned to many men in her life. Of course, she'd lay with them if they could meet her price, and a few, a very few, brought her to a climax. Ronnie Dixon was not one of those in her chosen sex life—a man to be with purely for the satisfaction they might derive from a romp in the hay with each other. But Ronnie Dixon was paying a large part of her bills and she never let on that she did not climax with him. Cynthia had learned all the tricks of the trade early in her youthful years. There were men and there were *men*. Then through experience along the Sunset Strip, she found there were some men who didn't look the part, but were more man than a truck driver when it came to being a bed partner. As it was with certain female types. Get a really good female into bed with another female and sparks can fly if the aggressor is any good at all.

When she met Glen on the freeway she had had a strange feeling which had bothered her for days. There was something strange about it she couldn't explain. After a couple of days she figured she would never see him again. And perhaps that was for the best, because Ronnie Dixon was due in nearly anytime for his regular visit. But Glen had stirred her imagination to the very core of her being. He had looked strong, yet had a delicate look in his thin frame. There was no doubt he was handsome—but again, handsome in the same delicate way. There was much more to that man than met the eye, and she wished she had been more forceful in letting him know she really did want to see him again. Something deep inside of the man had brought her to a self-gratification climax in her bed, alone, the same night she had first met him. It was something which had never happened to her before, and she wished it would never happen again. Her body was her business and she didn't like giving it away free even if it was to herself. For days after, she couldn't realize what had gotten into her, but the same thoughts and the same actions returned when she got into bed alone at night. The last night before Ronnie arrived she watched television late into the early morning hours. But it did no good. The same feeling was there, and Glen's face was there, and he was kissing her, rubbing his hands over her body, caressing the very fibre of her being. And then it was all over again and she went in to the bathroom to take a warm bath and change nightgowns...

Ronnie arrived Friday about noon. Cynthia hadn't gotten out of bed as yet, but he had his key. He came into her bedroom, and kissed her sleeping form. She moaned and turned over, still with the gathering thoughts of Glen in her sleep-filled mind. But she did not mention his name. She only groaned in ecstasy, and Ronnie thought it was for him.

There came an anxiousness over his body, a starved thing he knew everytime he laid eyes on the girl. And there she was before him in the bed, so sexy in the sheer pink nightgown, every curve, every secret of her body visible to his eye. Not that he hadn't seen it before, but each time he took the girl, looked upon her, there was the thought of new adventure. And Cynthia was the one to give it to him.

He took off his clothes rapidly, then felt the call for body relief and he went into the bathroom. He sat down on the commode and his eyes fell to the pile of blue nylon near the bathtub. He reached over for it and brought it to him. There were sections on the front of the gown which were hard. He put the garment to his nose and it detected the tell-tale odor. He slammed his body up from the toilet seat and threw open the door. He moved across the bedroom, grabbed the low slung front of the girl's pink nightgown and jerked her to a sitting position, still nearly asleep. He jammed the blue nightgown into her face.

"What in hell is this?"

Cynthia tried to mumble herself awake, but the shock had been too sudden. The realization would not come to her so quickly. But it didn't take her long to realize her benefactor was sitting on the bed beside her, and he was holding her nightgown front with one hand and the blue one of the night before in the other. He jammed the blue one into her face again, and his own face was red in anger, a red which was made more prominent by his silver-gray hair.

"What the hell is *this* all about?"

Cynthia tried to remain calm in the face of evidence which was only circumstantial. Then she got mad. "What in the hell is this all about?" she demanded in his own words.

"This!" He threw the blue nightgown into her face.

She knocked it to the floor, and slammed her legs over the side of the bed. "What right have you going into my laundry hamper?"

"The same right that I get from paying the bills around here, dear Cynthia."

She pulled her legs back up on the bed, then once more sunk down on the pillow. "How long has it been since you were here?" She found the routine which would please him.

"Too damned long, it would seem!"

"Three weeks, isn't it?"

"Three weeks to the day."

"And?"

"And you got somebody up here to practice your cheap tricks on..."

She snapped up on the bed. "Cheap! Brother, one thing you better know... I don't come cheap."

"My bank account will prove you out on that."

"Then take your bank account and shove it where it will do the most good for you." She flew off the bed and went into the bathroom where she slammed the door.

Ronnie, for about the third time in his life, felt silly racing across the room stark-naked, but it was too late to let that hamper him. He banged on the bathroom door which Cynthia had locked. "Open this goddamned door right now!"

"When you calm down, I might," she said and drowned out any further sound with the flush of a toilet.

The gray-haired man listened to the sound of

the rushing water and the ensuing sound as more water rushed in to replace that which was spent and realized, for the moment, he could not further his opinion. He walked slowly back across the room and sat on the edge of the bed, where he picked up the soiled blue nightgown, sniffed it once more, then tossed it across the room to the closed bathroom door. He felt completely sorry for himself. The amount of money he gave the bitch every month, and she would pull a dirty trick on him like that. "Dirty trick," he mumbled half-aloud. "Hell. I wonder how dirty the creep who had her was. Probably some young truck driver... or one of those bastards from the Strip she used to know."

Slowly he got up from the bed and went to the full-length mirror he had given her during Christmastime the year before. He looked hard at his image and didn't see much to be repulsed about. Not even much different from the time in his youth he had spent in the Marine Corps during World War II. There was a slight rippling at his belt-line and his hair had turned gray, but he was sound of limb and lung. Strange, he felt, how the other hairs on his body had not turned gray. Maybe that was pretty good too. He flexed his muscles, and felt pretty good again. There was something about flexing the muscles which always made him feel masculine at times when he was downcast. He flexed them again and smiled his approval in the reflected image, then turned to walk back toward the bed.

Cynthia waited a few moments, giving the man time to cool down, then cautiously opened the bathroom door and looked out to see him laying calmly back on the bed. She grinned, knowing the same old trick had worked again. He certainly wouldn't have broken down the door because the neighbors would have heard, and the one thing Ronald Dixon wouldn't want around were the cops. His wife in San Francisco would take that with the loving kindness of a bulldozer. But Cynthia knew from all her past experiences how far she could go. She felt she had gone far enough, and her attack was swift. She was going to race across the room and throw herself on top of the man who was supporting her so well. She pulled the bathroom door closed behind her and her feet made three swift steps forward, toward the bed, then got tangled with the nylon nightie Ronnie had thrown there.

She fell flat on her face. Her arm seemed immediately to dislocate. Ronnie came off the bed in all his nudity and fell to the floor beside her.

"Baby! Baby! Baby!" he cried, and he raised his arms around her.

Cynthia raised up on her good elbow and slowly rubbed the injured one. "It's not broken," she said softly.

Ronnie laid her back on the soft rug. "Just lay back. You'll be alright in a minute."

"You threw it there." Her voice was soft, but meaningfully determined for an answer.

"Yes... in a fit of temper."

"That's why you charged in the way you did. Temper. And you didn't even let me explain."

Ronald Dixon's eyes began to soften as he watched the girl put both her arms beneath her head. He knew the hurt had gone from her body, but he wanted to know the hurt had also gone from her mind. There was little for him to say but, "I'm sorry, darling…"

She rolled over to put an arm across his chest. Her smile permitted a wet tongue to cross his lips. "We know each other."

The words hit him wrong. He rolled over swiftly and captured the blue nightgown which he rolled back with in his hands. "And this is to let us know about each other?"

"Yes," she said softly, and her eyes looked into his with a sparkle he couldn't resist.

Ronnie leaned over and inserted his tongue between the lips which held no lipstick. He worked his mouth over hers for a longer time than he had intended. The manhood rose in his nakedness and he then rolled on top of her, but Cynthia was not ready for him. She kissed his earlobe, then his undefined nipples and let it ride to his navel base, then raced up to greet his lips again, at which point she rolled away, leaving him panting in his gasping for centered sexual abuse.

"You'll listen now," she said simply, and rolled away further from his searching arms. "Damn you!"

"Damn you!" he cried with the anguish of a lost soul.

"Three weeks, buster. Goddamn you! How long do you think a girl can take it without a romp in the hay? You can stay away three weeks and expect there should not even be a thought of bed life? Well I don't live it that way. When I want it, I want it now, and I've got to have it. You've known that part since the Goddamn day you met me. Sure, you foot most of the bills. But how can you foot a little jazzin' if you're out of town? I'm a girl who wants it, needs it and likes it. And any time you don't like the arrangement, you just get the hell out. Don't think you're the only one who will pay and pay plenty for the pleasures my body and my lips can give out. Maybe even I'd take on a lesbian if I thought about it, and she happened to be on the right spot at the right time."

"Don't talk like that," the little man whispered."

"I'll talk any way I damned well please and you'll listen to what I damned well say! Now you take me as I am or you won't be around taking me in any way at all. I live my life the way I want. You get value received and you know it. Don't you be coming in here after you've probably jazzed every broad on your whole circuit. That's another thing. How many broads are you keeping? And don't tell me I'm the only one, the true love of your miserable life. You got a lust for girls, mister, and it's not a lust that is satisfied once every two or three weeks when you decide to get back here and shack up with me."

"Honestly, there is no one else but you." He was near tears.

"Go to hell!"

"There just isn't, that's all."

"Like hell! Look, I wasn't born yesterday. I know the score. And look at this. I don't care a damn if you have a hundred broads stacked all over the country. I see my doctor once a week whether I need it or not, so I'm not afraid you might transfer some of their crud to me. I won't be transferring it back to you, that's for one

85

damned thing. And you're a lousy lay, you know that. You should know it, I've told you plenty of times. And if you want any more mouth exercises you're going to pay double."

"Why are you so mad, darling?" He was nearly pathetic.

"Mad? Why am I mad? You come in here and accuse me of all sorts of things. You find my nightgown which is a little stiff and you toss it around like a madman. That's an expensive piece of material. And more than that, you toss it right where I can fall over it. I could have broke my neck, then what good would I be to you or anyone? Maybe that's what you had in mind. There's an easy way of getting rid of a mistress. A simple accident in the doorway of the bathroom. Bet the greatest mystery writers in the country never thought of a clean-cut murder like that before."

"You're talking nonsense…"

"I never talk nonsense." She snapped over and picked up the nightgown and threw it into his face. "Didn't you ever hear of a wet dream?"

Ronald Dixon rolled back against the bathroom door. He hid his face in the folds of the nightgown, and Cynthia could hear soft sobs coming from that area… and there was the slight shaking of the man's shoulders. She had told him off many times in the past, but that had been the first time she had hit him so hard with her words. No man likes to be told he is lousy in the hay. Of course, she had mentioned it before, but it had always been in some sort of a joking way and she tried to teach him new routines from her excellent background of such things. But that time she had laid him low and it hurt. She had never seen him cry before. Pout, sure... but cry... never. She had hurt him deep. And she certainly didn't want him pulling up stakes. He gave her plenty and she liked the high life. Actually she didn't have anyone on the string who would keep her the way Ronald Dixon did.

Cynthia was a smart girl, and smart enough to know she had better cool off the situation, or heat it up as the case might be, before she did lose everything. Slowly she got to her knees and crawled to him. She took the nightgown down from his face and as he looked at her through tear-stained eyes she wiped them on the nightgown.

She let her hands go between his legs and very soon she knew that anything she said from that point on would be taken as the present and the past words would soon be forgotten.

"Dry your tears, my darling... Cynthia is here... and Cynthia is so angry with herself that she would speak such things to you."

"Why did you, Cynthia?"

"Only because I was angry because you thought I was cheating on you. I wouldn't do that to you, love... you know I wouldn't do such a thing."

He put his arms around her shoulder and drew her head down to his chest. "Yes... I understand. I was so wrong. I was a little jealous, I guess. I can understand your anger, because I can understand my own anger." His eyes glistened as her lips and her tongue forced its way in between his tightly closed lips. And when they parted again, his eyes were even wider in their bashful look into the pure sex of her own. She let the robe fall open so that her naked body was exposed to his every glare. "Will you teach me something new, Cindy?"

"Whatever you want, my love."

Then she stood up and let the robe fall from her shoulder to the floor at her feet. "Just stay there a minute."

Ronald Dixon did as he was told. He moved slightly so that his back was against the wall next to the bathroom door. Cynthia opened the door and went into the bathroom where a moment later he heard the water in the tub running at full force.

It was several minutes before Cynthia again came into the bedroom. When she did, she reached over and took his hands in hers and urged him to his feet. He was aroused sufficiently already, so much so that all he wanted at that moment was to take her to the bed and have at it. But he had asked her for something new, and he would go through with it.

Cynthia led him into the bathroom and when she had turned off the water she helped him into the tub where she soaped him down, every inch of his body. Then she wetted herself down and soaped her own body before she got into the tub on top of the man.

The warm water... the slippery bodies... the tongue-kissing beneath the surface of the water, the water running into each nostril, into the cracks left between their lips caused each to gag, but neither would come up for air, neither would stop the horror of ecstasy such a sensation caused... and her hand found his manhood and she moved it to the right position until they were as one. Only then did she remove the pressure of her lips and her head, and they came up over the surface of the water. Ronald Dixon gasped for breath for the first moment, but he could not stop the upward surge of his body into hers. And her downward thrusts made his gasps for air even more drastic. She did not want to drown him, but she loved the pain she was giving. The pain of animal sex. The water splashing over the side of the tub. The squishing sounds of their bodies. The force he tried as he kept his head above the water. And at that last moment when she knew he was about to explode, she jammed her lips against his. Her tongue darted in and out of his mouth. He wanted to take her in his arms and squeeze the life out of her but his hands were on the rim of the tub to keep him from going under.

To keep from going under was far from Cynthia's plan. She locked her lips in place and with all the power of her beautiful face and head she again forced the older man's head deep into the tub of water, and as they exploded through each other Ronald Dixon cried into her mouth under the water. The water filled his lungs in the same instant he exploded. He cried and cried but the only sound was the bubbles which exploded on the surface of the water. It was a horror of pain, of sex, of pleasure, of pure torture that he had never dreamed of, and she held him there until the last of his thigh-surging expense had drained itself. Then she let him up.

The man was dazed. He sputtered and spit and coughed, while Cynthia calmly got out of the tub and began to dry herself off. Finally he looked to her. "You wanted something new," she said.

The man gasped again... "I've never had anything so magnificent in my entire life... I've never... teach me, Cynthia... teach me and I'll be your slave for life... for life..."

"You are," she said simply.

Cynthia saw Glen as he walked into the Brown Derby. She wanted to race to him. She wanted to expound her body to him right there over the bar stool. It was more than she could stand trying to keep from simply racing up and grabbing him in her arms and shouting. "Thank God! Thank God you've come back!" And she could sense he felt the same way. As he approached their position at the table she realized only the fact Ronnie Dixon was a jealous man, and he was paying the bills. She tried her best to affix her eyes into some sort of a glare which could keep Glen away. She wanted him so much she could taste him, but she couldn't give up the luxury Ronnie afforded her. Then it became apparent as Glen passed by the table, without recognition, that he had gotten her silent message. And when he came back from the men's room she watched his ass as it moved rhythmically with each step. Then she thought she knew what it was. But it would take time. At the moment, all she knew was she wanted him and she was determined to have him. It was sort of like having one's cake and eating it too. But she was determined the time would come.

For more than an hour as Glen sat at the bar talking to the bartender she watched him. And she watched his face in the mirror, and she caught a glimpse of what she thought might be a point of anger, but she couldn't be sure from that distance. Then Ronnie had to go to the men's room and at that point it was all she could do to keep herself in check. She wanted to rush to the bar and take him in her arms, to let her hand race down the length of his body to a place where she knew his secrets were concealed. But she couldn't. Ronnie would be gone only a moment, and the nightgown bit would have been enough to assemble any other thoughts he might have and destroy her bank account.

Of course there was always the possibility Glen might have some money... But he didn't look it... and besides, she wouldn't want it from him. *There* was all in a man she could hope for. There was a strangeness about his walk, but that would have to wait for another time. She wanted him. She started to rise up from the table just as Ronnie returned to their table, and she sat down again.

She knew there had to be some way of contacting the man she knew she was in love with, even for a short time, and when it came to pass there was only one way. Ronnie didn't smoke. She took the lighter from her purse and flicked it several times, and it didn't light. Cynthia knew what she was doing. Ronnie didn't smoke. But she needed something to use to get across to Glen, some little note which would tell him her thoughts, her desires. And the maitre d' did exactly as she thought he would. He walked across the room to light her cigarette and leave the matchbook. It only then demanded her to await an appropriate moment to write the quick note she so passionately wanted to write. The opportunity came at the last moment as Ronnie stood up to pay the check. She dashed off the few words quickly with an eyebrow pencil.

Ronnie turned to adjust the angora stole around her shoulders, then side by side they started for the parking lot entrance to the Brown Derby. She made sure she was on the side closest to the bar, and as she passed where Glen sat, she caught his eye briefly in the mirror and she could see he knew something was up. There she dropped the matchbook, and it was little doubt he had seen the move.

But there was Ronnie and the long night ahead. A night she would give herself to him again as she had done so many times in the past, but a night she would be thinking of Glen.

CHAPTER TEN

L.A. POLICE INTERVIEW #1812 FILE—MARY KLAUS—SALESLADY

The Killer fitted the third pair of red, high-heeled shoes to his feet under a speculative look from the shoe saleslady. He got up confidently and once more paraded in front of the full-length mirror as he had done twice previously. He lifted his trouserlegs so as to better see the turn of his nylon-clad ankles, the only piece of feminity he wore except for the panties and brassiere under his outer male clothing.

After several long moments and steps in front of the mirror, he turned to the patient saleslady. "These will do fine," he said, then walked back to the fitting chair and sat down, where he calmly removed the shoes and handed them to the girl. At no time had he lost the seriousness of purpose, determination or features.

The girl gazed at her customer. Two things bothered her immediately. She wasn't quite sure if she should call him "Sir", or "Madam." And the shoes were $35.95. Her customer didn't look as though he could pay $5.95. However, she certainly didn't want to offend the customer. It had been a very bad week on Hollywood Boulevard for shoe sales. She needed every sale she could get.

As to watching a gaunt, not very good-looking man parading in front of her mirror wearing girls' shoes, well, when one had been in and around Hollywood as long as she had, the incident was nothing new. There had been a time when she was clerk in a ladies' clothing store and the boys would come in all the time and try on nearly everything she had in the store. And they were always good sales. Another thing she remembered: all of them without exception wore girls' panties. She couldn't help but wonder what color this guy was wearing. She figured him to be the sharp pink, or lavender type. Where he could show no beauty in his features, she visioned, he would try to show the beauty in the undergarments. But why red shoes? He certainly didn't appear to be the red shoe type; the red anything type. But that was none of her business. The sale was the most important thing, and it was apparent the sale was made.

The Killer paid her with a fifty dollar bill, and as she gave him the change, she said. "Come back again."

"I doubt it," he said as he fitted the shoebox under his skinny arm and left the shop.

WARDEN'S NOTE

The early evening air, cool with the coming of darkness, felt good against his face. He took several deep breaths, then hailed a taxi cab on the corner of Hollywood and Vine. His first thoughts were to get to his motel room and change. Pauline, in red, would make her debut to the Sunset Strip for the first time that night. It was certainly about time Glen should be showing up.

He'd had long enough to make the trip from Colorado. Too bad Glen hadn't gone to Chicago or New York. Those were the cities the Killer felt easier in. There was too much open space in Hollywood. Especially in the Hollywood area. There were none of the tenements or dark alleys where one could easily lose themselves if they chose. The job would have been so much easier had it been in one of those great cities. Besides, he knew them like the back of his hand. Hollywood was foreign, completely, to him. In the few days he had had, there was no real way of knowing the place. He would have to hit and run—run fast. Hide, and get out of town. And he *would* hit. The Syndicate did not hold for misses!

But it certainly was about time he ventured out onto the streets of the selected town in the attire in which he would do the job. He would become known as Pauline in several places, and in that way he could move about more freely. Once Pauline was known by the crowd she would be accepted without question. It was necessary to the overall plan... the overall plan for an assassination.

L.A. POLICE REPORT #9113—FRED HENT—BELLBOY—STRADER MOTEL

Pauline liked the red panties, brassiere and slip she had purchased earlier in the day. The red satin undies held their own purpose also. The red dress to be used was extremely sheer and at least the slip could be seen through it. At first she had nearly decided upon black. Seeing the undies through a sheer dress always made her feel sexy, so therefore it was only fact that the same sensations must be aroused in the eyes of any beholder. She had actually tried on the black ensemble under the dress, but the black showing through was much too startling. It would have to be a red. A deeper red than the dress so there would be some contrast, of course. The set of satin panties he selected he knew would be perfect, and he admired them as each one slipped so smoothly, delicately over his powdered skin. Then he took a long time in making up his face. The mascara was a very dark, almost black-blue, while the eye-shadow was a much lighter blue. The lipstick was an exact duplicate in red of the dress. And when he lowered the brunette wig into place, much of his homeliness disappeared. Of course there was little he could do with the oversized nose except to shadow it with the eye-shadow and add extra pink powder, but he was not the same as the ugly Paul. The dress slipped easily over her body as Pauline emerged again to the mirror for last minute adjustments and to comb the wig once more into place where the dress had disturbed a few hairs. Her earrings and necklace were gold-plated with red glass in them. She was indeed the lady in red as she slipped into her red cashmere wraparound coat.

Nothing remained of Paul except the hawk-like nose as she sat in front of the dressing mirror, waiting for the taxi she had called.

L.A. POLICE REPORT #616—TOM CONRAD —TAXI DRIVER

When the taxi came, the driver opened the

back door for her and with measured grace she got into the vehicle and was driven swiftly to Denny's Place on the Strip.

WARDEN'S NOTE AND COMMENT

A disreputable establishment known for its lesbian and homosexual crowd, most of the beatnik variety. But on more occasions than were countable, the sightseers, the curiosity seekers, the up-town crowd would go slumming. It was that particular crowd who paid the tab. Most of the beatniks had little or no money, but they gave the place its character and were tolerated by the owner, Denny, who in reality was a tremendous bull dyke who dressed in faded blue jeans, men's shoes and men's sweatshirts.

When Paul had investigated the Strip, he had found most of such places were run by the dykes or the transvestites who catered largely to their own crowd, but it was the tourist and the curious who really paid the bills. There were many coffee houses who catered to anyone who had the price and those seemed to be filled, especially on the weekends, with teenagers looking for some kind of a thrill. It was here that Paul had first sensed he could make a million dollars in such a short time if only he had some of the white stuff to peddle. But what he had to peddle was not for the teenage crowd, and he knew Glen/Glenda would not be hanging around teenager hangouts. It would be more to his liking in the gay bars. Paul liked the young stuff, the back alley trade, and he wished with all his mind that he was after a teenager instead of his present prey. Each time he had looked at the little broads with their youthful bubbles stretched against their sexy sweaters, and at short miniskirts which exposed their panties when they seated themselves, he wanted to rush to the nearest mirror with his full drag and have his own session.

But there was also the maniacal thought of putting on their clothes and having a session with them, as he had so many years ago in the parks and the schoolyard where he had killed in his lust for self-satisfaction. It was at such times, when his mind twisted in that direction, he had to fight with all his faculties to keep from completing his desires. Perhaps an opportunity would present itself for such desires. But first came the Syndicate and their demands. If he sacrificed their demands for his own satisfaction there would be hell to pay and he would find himself in Hell long before he had planned. Desires were one thing, but demands were another.

It was to the gay clubs Pauline directed her final and immediate attention. The younger crowds would have to wait for her attentions. And at Denny's place, the tall woman dressed entirely in red sat down in a far corner, a dark corner, of the establishment.

L.A. POLICE INTERVIEW #1212—
SHIRLEY CROSS—TOPLESS WAITRESS—
DENNY'S PLACE

The young waitress wore nothing but a black miniskirt and gold pasties over the nipples of her ample breasts. She wiggled them sexily as if she were enticing a man. But then, how could she know? Somehow she did, however. It seems when one works in such places any length of time they become attuned to the real and the unreal—the fact and the fiction.

"What do ya got on yer mind, dearie?" And she wiggled those fantastic boobies again. Then she grinned matter-of-factly. She let both her hands run down the sides of her breasts, then down along her hip line. "An' I bet these ain't part of what you got in mind, 'ceptin' iffn you'd like 'em growin' outta' yer own body." She giggled to the point the Killer wanted to kill her on the spot.

And with his deep masculine voice he imitated her little-to-be-desired vocabulary. "Iffn you got a Martini, or iffn you knows how to make one up, why don't y'all go over there to the bar an' do it?"

"Snotty bitch!" she said, then moved away, back toward the bar and the bartender who would do the actual fixings.

Pauline removed her red cashmere coat and draped it carefully over the back of her chair. She regarded the remark of the waitress as an insult, but thought little of it. There was too much else to be taken care of, and minor troubles such as that were little needed.

When the topless waitress returned with Pauline's drink she didn't further her earlier insult, but Pauline kept a heavy glare in her eyes until the girl left the area. But then the eyes were immediately drawn to the entrance door as a loud group of beatnik teenagers came in, loud and rowdy, and undoubtedly all were high on one form of dope or another. That alone was cause for alarm in the red dress-clad Killer. When dope, liquor and teenagers mixed it up there was bound to be trouble... trouble the Killer wanted no part of. Her masquerade would certainly come to light in trouble like that. Certainly if a bare-titted waitress could see through her make-up, so could the authorities. That wouldn't suit her purpose at all. The Syndicate didn't allow for failures under any circumstances. Her immediate instincts told her to get the hell out of the place and quick. But she took time to kill off her Martini, then took up the red cashmere coat and slipped into it. The couple of minutes delay were just long enough.

Three uniformed sheriff's men and three plain-clothes deputies entered. For a long moment they stood just inside the doorway as they surveyed the interior. Hard eyes. All-seeing eyes. And they were not missed by the eyes of the young people who started catcalls and jeers. The deputy in charge made a simple movement of his hand and all but one officer, who remained at the door, went into action, gathering the beatniks into one section at the side of the bar.

Pauline, knowing it was her only chance, sat down again at the table and silently toyed with the empty Martini glass; her eyes held steady on the action as the search procedure began.

L.A. POLICE INTERVIEW #1213—DENNY PRICE—OWNER—DENNY'S PLACE

Denny, the bartender-owner, leaned far across the bar to the deputy in charge. His eyes burned in the sudden dryness of mixed fright and irritation.

His place had been rousted before, but there was no doubt he'd never get used to such a situation. The possibility always existed wherein the next time they might close him up—perhaps for good. The Sunset Strip was a changed entity since the early days when he had opened Denny's Place. The early days of Hollywood. The fancy night-club it was then, only at that time it was called The Big D. Denny's Place only came about after World War II and the decline of all big name nightclubs along the Strip. Denny changed the name as the nightclub became less and less an elaborate affair and the clientele of the Strip became less and less human.

"I didn't sell them any liquor," Denny said in all sincerity. "And no beer, either. Ask any-body."

"Nobody said you did, Denny." The Deputy in charge did not look to him; rather he kept his eyes on the searching procedure, never missing a move.

"Look, Terry." Denny came around the edge of the bar and stood beside Terry, the Deputy. "My door is unlocked from eleven a.m. until two a.m. How in hell can I regulate who comes through it?"

"Nobody said you could, Denny." The Deputy Sergeant still didn't take his eyes from the search action and the giggling beatniks.

Pauline sat deep in her chair. She watched and she listened, but most of all she waited. Some kind of an opportunity had to present itself and Pauline would be ready to act upon it instantly.

The words came to her from far off across the room. But they were clear.

"Knives. A .32. Fingernail files, sharpened to a razor edge. Four sets of iron knuckles. You want me to go on Sergeant?" The uniformed Deputy had put the collection of violence on the bar.

The Deputy Sergeant looked to his brother officer with callous, knowing eyes. "Deputy! Haven't you heard the new ruling on search and seisure? This sort of thing can't be done any longer." But his eyes were narrow as he looked to the weirdly dressed characters with their hands on the wall, high over their heads. "No conviction," he mumbled.

The uniformed Deputy indicated the array of death-dealing equipment on the bar. "Yeah," he grinned knowingly. "But that's a lot of heavy crap that will find its way to the bottom of Terminal Island Harbor the next time we sink the hardware."

Terry matched the man's grin, then slapped him on the broad shoulders. "You got a point there, Ed." He looked to the prisoners. "There is something I'm supposed to inform you about. It's all about your civil rights."

The tallest of the group who supported a straggly beard and a Castro hat over cruddy, dark, long hair snapped a saliva-encrusted interruption. "We know all about our civil rights, copper!" Then he laughed. It was a nasty laugh. "You wanna tell us about it? Or do we tell you?"

Terry wanted to slug the creep, but that was just what the character wanted. Terry was a good cop and he wasn't about to fall into such a trap. He went through the civil rights bit slowly while the gang jeered him on, then he turned to the other officers. "Pack 'em in the wagons and get them the hell off the street."

The last to be ushered out was the tall, bearded youth who once more turned on Terry. "There's a thing goin' on on this Strip, cop and maybe one of these days somebody's gonna be jammin' *you* into a car."

"I've been on the Strip beat a long time, boy, and nobody's jammed me into a car yet."

"There's always a first time."

"The guy that tries it better be mighty big."

"The movement will be big alright... mighty big." Then a Deputy hustled the laughing character from the establishment.

Terry looked to the closed door a moment, then turned to let his eyes roam over the interior once more. They landed on Pauline, who fiddled with the empty glass. It made her nervous, but she kept her eyes on the big Deputy. There could be no doubt in anyone's mind that Pauline looked well over twenty-one. However, the all-red outfit did give her more than just a passing appearance of being a streetwalker. Terry took in the full of her for a long time. But there was nothing he could tag her for, except her looks, and you can't hold somebody for their looks. He once more looked to Denny, who had returned to his position behind the bar.

"Keep them out of here, Denny!"

"Now just how in hell am I going to do that, Terry?"

"You might get off cheaper if you hired a bouncer. You take enough off the gay crowd, without catering to the other creeps." Terry didn't

103

wait for the protests he knew would be forthcoming. Denny ran a gay bar and he knew Terry knew it. But there were more important things on the Strip than the gay crowd. He had felt something building there for a long time, but he couldn't put his finger directly on it. But when a man has had a beat that long he can feel when something is wrong. Something was very wrong and it wasn't the gay crowd.

Terry let the door swing shut behind him.

L.A. POLICE INTERVIEW #1212—
SHIRLEY CROSS—TOPLESS WAITRESS—
DENNY'S PLACE

Pauline breathed a sigh of relief as the topless waitress crossed to her and put a fresh Martini on the table.

"Close, huh?"

Pauline looked up to the girl. "I didn't order that."

"Thought you might need it."

"What makes you think that?"

"That was Terry Mahoney. Toughest fuzz on the Strip."

"So?"

"It's a good thing he wasn't on the prowl for little boys in girls' clothes." She grinned and went back to the bar.

CHAPTER ELEVEN

L.A. POLICE INTERVIEW #999—CYNTHIA HARLAND

Ronald Dixon didn't stay the night. He wanted to. He drove Cynthia Harland back to her apartment with all the intentions of staying the night and getting an early start in the morning, but it hadn't worked out that way. Cynthia's mind was centered on Glen and the ride she wanted from him. Her mind remained at the Brown Derby while her body faced Ronnie, who poured himself a stiff jolt.

He kissed her twice, then with little or no response from the girl he sat his glass down on the bar and started to remove his trousers. The move brought Cynthia out of her daydreams. "Not tonight, Ronald."

He looked at her amazed. His eyes went wide. "Not tonight? What kind of talk is that?"

"My period just started."

"You were alright a few hours ago."

"It just started." She got up and moved to him, then put her arms around his neck and kissed him briefly. "You'll be down again next week, honey. Everything will be alright by then."

"I won't make it for three weeks. I've got to leave for Washington. I want you bad, honey."

"You know how I am this time of the month. We'll just have to postpone it. There's

105

nothing I can do, Ronnie."

The man reluctantly fastened his belt again, then took his drink down in one gulp. "You sure you haven't got somebody else coming in?" He indicated the bathroom. "I still remember the nightgown."

Cynthia shrugged as she poured a quick drink for herself.

"Stay and see for yourself. I'm not telling you you can't stay. I'm just saying, there is nothing I can do for you tonight." The entire statement was a lie, but she simply didn't want another affair with the man. She wanted to be fresh and alive for Glen when he arrived in the morning. She didn't want to have any memories of the older man and his miserable idea of a jazz session.

Ronnie looked at the back of her head studyingly for a long moment, then he sighed and tried for a smile. It was a weak smile of disappointment, but he said: "Alright, honey. If that's the way it is, that's the way it is. If you had somebody coming in you certainly wouldn't want me staying around."

"All I want to do," she said as she turned to face him, "is to get out of this tight dress, into a satin nightgown and get some sleep. You know I had four days at the studio this week, and they were long days. That's probably what brought my period on so suddenly, that and your jazz earlier. I'm tired out."

"Sure, Cindy... sure. I know how it is." He put on his suit jacket then reached to the inside pocket where he took out a billfold. He counted out several bills and laid them on the bar. "You'll need some things while I'm gone, and the rent will be due before I get back."

She brought his head down to hers and her hot tongue darted in between his lips. He drew himself tighter to her and she felt his manhood rising rapidly. She pulled slowly away, keeping a warm glowing smile on her face. "You're so good to me, Ronnie."

Ronnie crossed his legs hurriedly. He had to hurt himself in order to lower his heat-excited body before he could walk. Cynthia knew his problem, so she lifted her drink to his lips and he gulped some of the stinging liquid. "Good night, Ronnie," she cooed.

Silently he walked to the door and without looking back again, he was gone.

Cynthia giggled silently, then reached behind her to unfasten a hook. She pulled down the zipper and let the dress fall in a circle about her feet where she left it. For a brief moment as she finished her drink she thought about taking a bath, but she found she was tired, and the sooner she went to bed and fell asleep, the sooner time would pass and she would know the real secrets of the man who would possess her. She let the strapless slip and brassiere fall on top of the dress, then walked into the bathroom to select a nightgown. She took a long time in selecting just the right one from a wardrobe of many. After all, she knew she would still have it on when Glen arrived in the morning. It had to be just right, and the matching negligee had to flow in billowing clouds.

But even after she was between the ivory satin sheets and the light was turned off, sleep did not come easy. Glen's handsome face haunted her

107

conscious mind. Her hips moved rhythmically with anticipation. She suddenly crossed her legs hard. It had to be saved for Glen. Everything had to be saved for Glen.

CHAPTER TWELVE

GLEN MARKER'S CONFESSION—TAPE

I sat in the bar of the Brown Derby until I felt the place closing in on me. Its soothing, dim lights and the many double Martinis had my vision swimming, but the note Cynthia had left me remained clear. I had not folded it again since the moment I'd picked it up from the floor. I studied every letter of the lovely handwriting. There was no doubt she wanted me, and I wanted to be with her right at that moment. I found myself hating the fact she was with another man, and the thoughts of her naked in bed with the guy brought fire to my neck. I hadn't been so close to wanting the death of someone in many months.

"I don't even know the broad," I realized to myself. "Why would I want her guy out of the way like that? Out of the way maybe, but not out of the world."

Then I found myself grinning at my thoughts.

"First time I've seen you smile in hours," said the bartender as he brought another double.

"First time I've felt like it in hours," I grinned, then pulled the Martini in close, and toyed with the glass stem.

I finished off the cocktail quickly, paid my tab and with a friendly goodnight to the helpful bartender, I left the Brown Derby and walked to the curbing where I hailed a taxi and soon found myself back in the hotel room. I looked several times at the whiskey bottle on my nightstand, but better sense kept me from taking any. Whiskey and gin didn't mix and I knew it.

Perhaps I was whiskey and Cindy was gin. How would we mix? It appeared she wanted me, and I was certain I wanted her. But just how would the two of us mix it up together?

I slipped a pink nylon nightgown down over my naked body then put my body prone on the bed with my hand under my head. I stared up at the ceiling without turning off the lights. The glow of the gin shot distorted pictures on the ceiling, but they were all of Cynthia. I quickly erased any thoughts of the gray-haired man she was with, but even at those times I realized I was a newcomer on the scene. Cynthia was a beautiful girl and she must have many men friends. I was lucky to possibly be included. But again, how would we mix?

I let my hands slip momentarily down the length of my body, over the soft nylon of the nightgown. "What will she think about this?" I questioned myself, half aloud.

My mind raced back to Colorado and Red. She had been one hell of a girl; there were many times I missed her. Red had gone for me no matter what I wore. But always I remembered the Syndicate, and they would be looking for me. I had to get out of the country as soon as possible. There was still the fact I wanted the operation which would kill my manhood once and for all, which brought up a thing that troubled me greatly. How would it really be when I was a girl? I had a great love for sex with girls. But when the operation made me a girl, there would be no girls for me, unless I went to lesbian love, there would have to be men. Of course there had been a few in my past, but they just weren't my cup of tea. I knew that girls' clothing was the only real love in my life, thus I wanted the operation which would make me as much a girl as possible. It was the entire reason I had broken with the Syndicate in the first place. But what of my sex life then? What of a different kind of sex life than I had ever known? I felt I would be a good-looking girl. After all, when I was dressed completely as Glenda, the mirror certainly told me I lacked nothing for looks. The operation I demanded of myself couldn't change my outward facial appearances. But would the operation change my mind in any way? Could it possibly bring me to the fact that I would forevermore be with men?

If there was to be any time with Cynthia, she would have to know. I had always heard that the movie people were attuned to all sorts of people. And Cynthia was with the movies. She'd understand. I hoped she would understand. But if she didn't... then it was just so much water over the hill. Tomorrow would tell the story. Tomorrow would tell just how long I would remain in Hollywood. What the hell! I could come up with a phoney birth certificate for my passport. That was also something I would need—a passport. Never having had one, I didn't know how long it would take, so the sooner I got onto it, the sooner I could take off when the time came.

Sleep came hard for me. But when it came I slept soundly with the light on, and when morning came it was one of the gray mornings

111

Californians had grown to know and accept.

I slipped lazily out of the pink nightgown and let the cloud of material drift across the bed where it would remain. I shaved very close and showered thoroughly, then drenched my body in a light cologne before I dressed.

Moments later I was in a taxi heading for Cynthia's apartment on the Sunset Strip. Her note had said to call, but what the hell? If she wanted me, she'd take me the way I came. So it wasn't noon. It was only ten in the morning. But it would be closer to eleven by the time I got there. The guy would have to be gone by that time, if she wanted me to call at noon.

I rang the bell on Cynthia's door at ten-thirty. I rang it several times before a sleepy voice from the other side asked: "Who is it, please?"

"Glen. Glen Marker."

"Oh!" It was a gasp and for a moment I thought the guy might still be there. But a moment more and her lovely voice spoke again. "Just a minute, Glen. Let me get a negligee on."

I couldn't hear her move off, but I knew she had gone from the immediate vicinity of the door. She wasn't gone long. I braced up quickly when I heard the night-latch being taken off and the door opened.

"Hi," I greeted with my best grin.

"Hi," she answered with an inviting smile.

Then there was a long pause as we looked into each others eyes. Finally I made a futile motion with my arms. "Do I come in, or do I stay out in the hall?"

"Oh, I'm sorry," she cooed and backed away from the door. "Come in Glen, please come in."

I moved swiftly, and she closed and locked the door behind her. Then she leaned back against the door and watched me as I moved across the deep carpet of the apartment. I turned again to face her as I reached a white, fur-covered divan.

"You're as beautiful as I remembered you," I reflected.

"And you must still be blurry-eyed from the Martinis you were drinking last night. I haven't even washed my face or combed my hair." She let her hands run up the side of her hair.

"Beauty is in the eyes of the beholder."

"So it would appear. I thought you were going to call me at noon." She slowly started to cross toward me.

"That's what your note said, not what I said. Besides, this way was much faster."

She stood directly in front of me, the fragrance of her perfume drifted out through the pink nightgown and negligee, and I thought quickly of my own pink nightgown which lay on the bed back in my hotel room. Soon the house woman would be in to make up the bed, and there it would be. So what? So I had had a girl with me! I laughed at the thought.

"Something funny?"

"Yes."

"Not me, I hope."

"Of course not. Maybe sometime I'll tell you."

I reached down and gently pulled her head to me. She did not resist. Rather, she lifted her own arms and drew me tightly to her, and the kiss was long, and wet, and hot. Our tongues met, and I liked the feeling of her lipstick smearing over my own lips, and the soft velvet of her tongue searching out each taste bud.

When we parted I let my hands slip down to fit over her snug hips, and she followed my move with her own. "Who are you, Glen Marker?" she breathed as she buried her head on my chest.

"Just a guy you met on the road."

"That goes double." I lifted her head again and our lips and open mouths met again.

"I get the idea," she sighed when once more we parted.

"I got it hours ago," I grinned. "Who was the guy last night?"

"I told you I'm a kept woman."

"So you did. Did he stay last night?"

"I got rid of him."

"You should have let me know."

"How? Besides, I didn't know I was going to get free. He can be difficult about such things sometimes."

"I bet he can."

"He's a lousy lay."

I wasn't sure if I liked her direct approach. But what the hell? She was a lovely piece if I'd ever seen one. "You sure don't pull your words, do you?"

"Should I?"

"Not that I can see."

"Time is so short. Who wants to beat about the bush? I don't care where you came from, Glen Marker, you must have heard that the Hollywood crowd is a fast crowd. Now tell me that you didn't."

"If I did I'd be lying through my teeth."

Our lips pressed, fused together again. Our

bodies melted as if into one. I realized immediately that everything she boasted up front was absolutely real, and in the same thought I let my right hand drift smoothly, easily down into the front of her nightgown. The soft globe which supported a hard nipple greeted my hand with the warmth of promise and I squeezed it tightly; first one, then the other, until the girl moaned with the delight of expectancy.

"Take your clothes off," she muttered through our tightly pressed lips. "Now! Now! Take them off!"

I didn't like to be naked with my women. I wanted a nightgown; some kind of girls' wear. It gave me, always, that extra stimulation I demanded of myself. But how could I go about it?

Without taking my lips from hers, my searching tongue explored hers. I unbuckled my trousers and let them fall to the floor. Then she unbuttoned my shirt with searching fingers. She did not look to what she was doing. Her lips were still fused to mine, her eyes closed. Then her groping hand felt me through the thin, pink nylon panties I wore.

Her eyes snapped open. But she did not jerk either her hand or her lips from mine. It was a slow movement. First her lips drifted a few inches from mine and she looked down. "Oh no," she sighed. "Don't tell me I've hungered this long only to be cheated."

"Only if you want to be cheated," I remarked seriously.

Then she removed her hand. "I'm from Hollywood, remember," she replied. "I know about such things."

115

"Then you should know what I am."

She turned from me and made her way to the bar. "I go to the bars on the Strip."

"What's that got to do with it?"

"Whiskey?" she asked without looking back to me.

"It's kind of early!"

"It's never too early in Hollywood."

"Good. Then if whiskey is what you're having, whiskey is good enough for me."

She poured two straight shots and brought one back to me. "I go to the gay bars once in a while."

"Then you should know the difference between a transvestite and a momosexual."

"Just how gay are you?"

"Why don't you wait and find out?"

She eyed me carefully, then downed her whiskey. "I know the facts... the difference. I know the butch girls, the gay girls, the stags, the street trade. You name it and I know it. I don't know any drags that go for girls—real girls, I mean. I don't know any that can give satisfaction guaranteed. Oh, some talk a good game. They get up here and all they want to do is lay around in my clothes." She waved her hands in frustration as she walked back to her bar and poured another straight shot. "All night I thought about you. I've had it with guys like last night. I sure expected something out of you." She laughed. "And there you stand in your panties. Man oh man, am I about ready for the rubber room at the happy farm!" She slugged her whiskey again and poured another.

I didn't touch my drink. I walked across the

room and put it on the bar, then walked back to where my trousers lay. I reached over and started to put them on. "There I stand in my panties." I said.

She snapped around. "Why do that? You might just as well go all the way. You look like my things might fit. I even have a few wigs on the dresser in my bedroom. There's two closets full of clothes in there also, and the dresser has all the little dainties you'll need underneath. You see, I come fully equipped for all my trade." She had tried for anger. It wasn't working.

But I had taken enough. I crossed to her and slapped her a resounding blow across the face. The smack knocked her first against the bar, then she spun off and landed in a white, fur-covered chair. For a long moment the girl was dazed, then her hand went to the sore spot on her cheek. "I've never taken that from anybody."

"You just took it, baby! Nobody laughs at me!"

"I never took that from anybody. But there's never been a drag that's done that before."

"What you have on will be good enough."

"What?"

"Just what I said. I don't need to see your closets. Maybe a wig. But the nightgown and negligee will be enough for the time being."

Dazed, she leaned forward in her chair. "I only wanted a good romp in the hay. I had planned so hard on it."

"I won't be laughed at!"

"I didn't mean to laugh. It was all disappointment. I honestly didn't mean to laugh."

I reached for the bottle and poured a second shot into my glass on the bar, then I tossed in a

117

piece of ice which I took from a small refrigerator behind the bar. The stinging but cool liquid, took some of the red from my face. "I certainly meant to dip you."

She rubbed her cheek. "That's apparent."

Slowly, Cynthia got to her feet and crossed to the bar. There was something puzzlingly different about the man who stood there. She had never been a masochist or a sadist in all her life, but for some strange reason she didn't mind the hard slap from this guy. There was something she couldn't understand. It was so easy to read her thoughts.

I eyed her a long moment, then reached over and poured her another drink. "This may take some of the sting out of your cheek."

Cynthia took the drink. "Hope it takes the black out of a black eye. I can't work all week if you gave me a black eye."

"You won't have a black eye. I know where the punch is to land."

"Professional?"

"You might say that."

"Professional lady-smasher?"

"Among other things."

"You don't look that way either."

"But I do look homosexual?"

She blushed deeper in red than the spot where the slap had brought a rush of blood under the skin. "Your panties caused that remark." She let her hands rub over my bare chest.

"Your chest should tell me different."

"But it doesn't, is that it?"

"I don't know. It's strong enough." She looked up into my eyes again. "You... you're certainly built there... you might be... you might be different."

"Want me to take my pants off again?" I was determined in my love and in my words. It wasn't so much that I wanted to get into her pink nightgown and negligee; after all I had one at the hotel which was almost its duplicate except for the material. I would have preferred something else. But pure determination held me by the groin and I knew the sooner I got something of hers on and did something for her, the sooner the girl would know she had a tiger by the tail.

"Will you go through with it?" She turned her eyes away from me again and picked up the drink from the bar.

"You think I won't?"

"Most of them don't."

"I'm not most."

"Nightgown and negligee?"

"While your body heat is still in them."

"That helps?"

"In a way."

"What way?"

"Why do you keep talking? Why don't you just wait and see. Lay down and enjoy it. Pull out the stops and go at it. Like you said before, time is too short. Now is the time and here is the moment. You want to spot the action, or just talk about your lost love affair?"

"And if I don't like it?"

"I put on my pants and go home. You put on your nightgown and negligee then go back to bed and have a good cry."

"You're awful. You even hurt with your words."

"You'll never know until you try."

119

"Want a drink first?"

"I have one." I unbuckled my trousers and let them fall to the floor in front of the bar and once more I faced her in my pink panties.

She looked to me slowly. "They're almost the same color as my nightgown and negligee."

"They're not satin."

"That matters?"

"Not really."

She slinked out of the negligee and let it drift over one of the three barstools. Her eyes never left mine and I could see she felt my own heat building. All she had to do was look downward to my pink panties and she would know it. She took another sip of her drink, then let each dainty strap of her nightgown come free of her shoulder and the nightgown fell to her ankles where she stepped out of it. She let her right foot come up slowly and the nightgown remained hooked over her pink fur-covered mules. I unfastened it and quickly let the gown slip over my naked body. I hoisted the negligee and my arms easily found the sleeves. I tied the long streamers tightly at my neckline, and even without the wig I knew the transformation was astonishing to her.

Glenda watched Cynthia remove her own pink panties. "They match the outfit," she said and handed them across.

Glenda slipped out of the nylon panties and put the pink satin ones on in their place.

"What do you call yourself?" asked Cynthia quietly, her eyes narrowing in the burning lust she had begun to feel.

"Glenda. Glenda Satin."

"Satin. It goes so well. Glenda Satin, in satin."

"The professional part I was telling you about."

"It fits. I have satin bed sheets."

"We'll get to them." She grinned. "Perhaps more often than you think right now."

"I'm looking forward to it. But I'm not counting on anything right now." But her eyes belied her inward emotions. Her breath had shortened, and she wet her lips much more than was necessary. Glenda knew from that moment Cynthia had been with girls before, and she would again. She went with men, and she went with women. After all, Cynthia had implied it all herself. She was a professional in her own right. The one who could pay the highest was her man for the night, no matter what sex they might be.

L.A. POLICE INTERVIEW #999—CYNTHIA HARLAND

Glenda reached up to pull her head down again, but the kiss was short-lived. Cynthia put her arm around Glenda's waist and led her into the bedroom where, a moment later, she had adjusted a blonde wig to Glenda's head then stood back breathing in eager anticipation.

No matter what Glenda looked like in drag, she was strong. She reached over and picked Cynthia up bodily and carried her to the rumpled satin sheets and carefully put her down. Then they were together, and their lips were once more fused together. The time was at hand and the kaleidoscope of colors started between them almost immediately. Cynthia knew from the outset she had been wrong. She had almost let

121

Glenda go without a try. Glenda was like none of the others. There was a color to her Cynthia never knew, not the black and white of most drags. Perhaps she had been wrong about some of the others she had let drift out of the apartment in past months. Glenda was near perfect. The soft lips on her breasts, the biting teeth on her nipples, the investigating hands which found every facet of her body. And when those hands found the facets they turned them on full force. There was the tip of a tongue hitting her navel base and the valley of untold secrets. There were the hands which ventured into her navel base and the valley of untold secrets. There were the hands which ventured into the unknown and came back with all the pleasures of Shangri La... and the kaleidoscope of color and sound burst forth with organ music which drifted from wall to wall, then repeated itself until the resounding sounds burst from the bed to the ceiling, then melted through the bed and bounced back from the floor. A ringing slammed into her ears and she wanted to hear the ringing over and over again until it would burst her eardrums.

Her hands clawed into real skin, taking with it bits of satin strands that could never be replaced. She didn't want anything replaced. All she wanted was Glenda and her searching tongue, fondling hands and violently thrusting manhood.

The pink clouds opened up and the blue sky threatened to overtake them both. But the thunder and the lightning blasted forth with a force she had never experienced. Her eardrums broke and there was only silence as the colors melted into a glowing darkness.

If she was dead Cynthia knew she had died happy. But she was not dead. The pleasure-hurt remained too long after the silence and the darkness had closed in. And she felt the stilled body so pleasantly heavy over most of her body. Only dreams remained...

GLEN MARKER'S CONFESSION—TAPE

Only dreams, for a longer time than either of us desired. It had been a rough tussle in which Glenda had become the violent aggressor. Glenda had to prove to Cynthia how wrong she had been. She would never say to Glen again: "There you stand in your pink panties." Never again would she think of me as a homosexual. From that moment on she would be looking forward to our next session. And those sessions would be frequent and demanding. But for the moment Glenda was pooped. She had fought so hard with every trick of the trade she had ever learned, used, or dreamed of, and she knew the girl beside her was satisfied to the fullest extent of her dreams.

"What do you think now?" Glenda finally found the breath to speak.

"Ummmmm," was all the girl could mutter. But her hand went to the tender spots between his thighs. Glenda still wore the panties, and the nylon was hot and moist. Her hand circled the soft nylon caressingly, left to right, right to left, up and down, and instantly she knew Glenda was once more aroused.

And Glenda tip-tongued the nipples of the girl's breast after she had lowered the strap of her

123

nightgown. The girl weaved slowly on the bed like a snake in heat, with little moaning sounds coming from her lips. They were both tired from the first jousting, but not so tired that the sensations of renewed life were not forthcoming. Glenda raised her bright red lips to those of the girl, and the girl whispered into her mouth. "Maybe some whiskey will help."

Glenda breathed the words back into the girl's mouth. "It would only kill things even more. Give it all time. Time will take care of all things... just give it time..." And she planted her moist, hot tongue deep in the hidden recesses of her mouth, her throat, and in return the girl let her own love maker circle round and round. The heat came on like a flash and the girl's hand continued it's movement in changing directions over Glenda's panties. "Oh baby," she moaned as she felt Glenda swelling and throbbing. Her own legs began to twitch in dainty little ripples, ripples she could not and did not want to deny. With her free hand she took Glenda's from her stomach and moved it down between her thighs where again it drifted through the valley and the meadows where only lust dwelt.

She had no panties on, but her skin was as moist and as hot as were the panties of Glenda. Glenda liked the feeling. There was so much the feeling of comfort and well-being, of still secrets which might be told. But Glenda knew that the male part of her would not completely respond for awhile. There was only one thing left to do... and she wanted to do it that way very much. She had never wanted to do it that way as much since the session with Red, so long ago in

Colorado, but Cynthia had so many of the qualities Red had had. And they were both professionals. Perhaps that made much of the difference. And in the same vein, she had rejected Glenda on first sight of the panties and chemise. Both, from past experiences, had been left with much to be desired from the drags they had met, but both soon learned there was a difference. Glenda wanted Cynthia that way, and she slowly pulled the nightgown up over the girl's body until it rested at the neckline just above the breasts. Once more she let her tongue dart over the nipples, then took the full mounds into her mouth and wished they were her own. She took such a long time with each of the breasts, making them moist and wet—so wet that her lips had a hard time keeping any form of traction, and the traction was so necessary for the full pleasure Glenda bit into first one and then the other, until the girl below screamed in pain, but she did nothing to pull the torturous instruments away. Instead she pulled Glenda's head even tighter to her, so tight that the hair of her wig fell to cover the entire upper portion of her body. She liked that feeling also. Many times she had been with lesbians, and even the ones who did have some sort of long hair never gave her the sensation that Glenda gave her.

Glenda let her tongue finally leave that portion of her body and it took a long time, so very long, in its slide down the length of her front. And when it was below the girl's navel she moaned... all the joys of a home run thrilled her. She never wanted to stop now, and she threw her thighs high in the air to meet every move. She had to meet every move or she would lose some of the pleasure.

And Glenda thrilled with every stroke. Soon, all too soon it would be over—at least for that moment. Then a little later it would be Glenda's turn. Throughout that portion of their session Glenda knew she had a tiger by the tail also, and she would know her business. Some pros were as bad as most amateurs... not so Cynthia. It was no wonder she lived in a three hundred dollar a month apartment, and Glenda knew the wardrobe would be one as expensive and in as good a taste as Glen had left in New York.

Perhaps it was not to the exact rules of the book that such thoughts raced through anyone's mind while in such a position, but it was those thoughts which gave Glenda all the power and sex-provoking demands which pleased any partner she might be with. Without the clothes, and without the thoughts, there would only be another set of flesh on flesh. Anybody could do that. It was the little deviations which made it all so worthwhile, so demanding that each would rather remain in bed than do anything else in the world. And there would be so many more nightgowns and negligees... Glenda was in a dreamworld.

CHAPTER THIRTEEN

L.A. SHERIFF'S DEPARTMENT—
OFFICERS' REPORT #1291—
DEPUTY SERGEANT TERRY MAHONEY

Terry Mahoney checked into headquarters just before eight o'clock that Saturday night. He went through his regular routine, then before checking out a squad car, he stopped in the ready room for a cup of coffee which he had just started to pour when a uniformed officer came in.

"Just looking for you, Sergeant."

"What's up?"

"The Chief wants to see you. He's in his office." Terry nodded his acceptance of the order, but took his time in drinking the hot coffee. Then he ambled his way through the sub-station to his superior's office. He didn't bother to knock; those formalities were left to polite actors in motion pictures. If the chief wanted to see him, then the chief damned well wanted to see him and there would be few formalities.

Terry's superior was a man almost as big as Terry himself, and as if the police department lived on coffee, the man was sipping from a big mug which he replaced to his desk as Terry came in.

"Want some coffee?"

"Not now, Claude. Just had one."

The Chief lit up a long cigar. "What'd it look

like to you on the Strip last night?" He blew out the first gust of smoke. "Same as usual to you?"

"Nothing's been the same as usual for weeks."

"That's the report I get. How many of the punks do you think are roaming the Strip these weekends."

Terry seated himself in a large leather chair near his superior's desk. "Thousands. Maybe more. Never did stop to count them. Just one big mob. We've had them in here from all over. Pasadana. Pacific Palisades. North Hollywood. Ventura. Bakersfield. Palmdale. You name it, and those characters come from it and right here to our little old Strip. Dirty clothes. Long hair. Sweaters that even the Salvation Army wouldn't accept. And most of them teenagers. You get them secondhand, Claude. I'm out in the field, remember." Terry folded his hands over his stomach.

"You and I both know that anybody who wants to can buy anything they desire on the Strip. One connection leads to another. And the connections aren't hard to find. Hard to find? Ha! They go out and drum up their trade these days. We pick up one and there are fifty to take his place." The big man leaned forward in his chair and put his elbows on the desk. "This LSD craze is going to cause us a lot of trouble. It's going to put a lot of those kids in the cemetery."

The chief nodded his head. "But before it does they are going to be taking such trips as we couldn't realize." He leaned back in his chair again and his eyes narrowed. "Matt and Rale were attacked by about ten of them last night. All hopped up on the stuff. We got most of them, and will get the rest. But ten is a gang..."

"Two can be a gang."

The chief nodded again. "Sure. Two. Three. Ten. I don't think it's going to stop at ten."

"A mob."

"And more."

"That's a riot you're referring to, Claude."

"That's what I'm referring to. It happened in Watts, and it can damned well happen here. Somebody wants trouble on the Strip. And by God, they'll do everything in their power to see that trouble does happen!"

"That sounds political."

"Call it what you want, Terry. But my guess is it's more than a bunch of kids looking out for a wild time. The stuff is too easy for them to get. Couple of the punks we picked up last night never had the stuff before. Said they were talked into it. Then when they were on their trip they have no recollection of what happened. They could have killed Matt and Rale with their tire irons if the action hadn't been spotted by another of our prowl cars. There is much more to it than a few pushers trying to get the kids hooked, thereby having another client. Most of those kids don't have the cash for their espresso, let alone lay out the kind of cash the stuff costs."

"I grab 'em everytime I get a chance. But the new 'hands off' laws aren't making it any too easy."

"I know... I know, Terry. We've got to be careful. But we've got to protect our own first. And don't take any chances with the girls either. They're as bad as most of the boys. And a hell of

129

a lot of the time you'll find the girls are in reality boys. They put on the capris, and the fuzzy sweaters, and with the long hair—who can tell? You'd even have a hell of a time getting them for masquerading. They don't wear falsies, or if they do they get rid of them before being searched. And they don't wear panties. They don't wear nothing. That goes for the real girls. They get flying high and don't even want to take time in lowering their panties. They lift their skirts behind one of those saloons and have at it standing up. These days you can't tell one from the other. It's their constitutional right to dress just about as they damned well please. The only way you're going to tag anything on them and make it stick is if they're disturbing the peace."

"That's not hard to grab 'em on. I've been around a long time. Lots of things constitute disturbing the peace."

Claude puffed heavily on his cigar. "Which is just about what I mean. Grab 'em. Only grab the ones who are on a trip. I want to know more about it. I want to find out just what is going on. I didn't like what happened last night. It's the first time any of them went that far, at least out here in our territory."

And Terry leaned back thoughtfully, remembering the threat he had so recently received. They would be pushing him into a car one of these nights, and Terry knew the creep had meant it. He leaned forward in his chair again. "I know what the bums look like when they're traveling on that stuff. I've seen them enough."

"I know you do, Terry. But I don't want any of my men traveling alone for a while."

"I've handled the Strip, alone, in my car, for a damned lot of years."

"That's an order. You have anybody in particular you'd like traveling with you for the next few weekends?"

"They're all good men."

"Gilboy. Do you know Don Gilboy?"

"By sight, nothing more."

"Young fellow. I've had him prowling the joints as one of the crowd. Take him with you tonight. He might be able to point out some of the creeps you don't know, some of them who are real tight on the stuff."

"You're the Chief."

"The businessmen on the Strip like you. But don't take any chances you don't have to. Their buck in the pocket always seems to come out way ahead of friendship."

"Most of the slobs I'd like to see right here in the lock-up." Terry stood up. "Anything else?"

"Only to repeat that I don't like what happened last night. Keep your eyes wide open tonight. And remember what I said about the girls and the girls who only look like girls. You know the gay crowd; you can differentiate between the gay crowd and the muggers and the slobs."

"I know them."

Terry closed the door almost silently, then checked out his vehicle. He knew Gilboy and would pick him up at one of the Strip dives along old Sunset Boulevard.

And as he drove along the gaily lighted Boulevard he couldn't help but think what the greats and the near greats would say if they could come back from Heaven, or wherever, and look at the street of *their* playtime as it stood now.

Where once all the fabulous nightclubs expounded their bright lights and great talent there was little more than creaky joints which shouted of topless waitresses, pizza, and beer. There had always been the gay bars where the homosexuals of both sexes gathered. But there had never been the joints where the kooky crowds gathered, or the beatnik joints which called loudly for the teenagers from all over the countryside.

Other than to squelch a fist-fight between a Bogart and somebody who wanted to take him, or small fights between starlets, there had never been the mass arrests he had witnessed and been a party to during the recent months. "What would they say?" he mumbled half aloud, then saw Don Gilboy ambling along the street near Denny's Place.

Terry pulled the car out of traffic and with the motor running he stopped near the disguised officer. "Gilboy," he called softly.

The younger officer looked to the car, then crossed to it. "Hello, Sergeant."

"The Chief says for you to ride with me tonight."

Without another word the young officer got in beside Terry, and the Sergeant put the car into motion again back into the steady stream of traffic. "Anything buzzing?"

"Something, Sergeant. But I can't lay my finger on it yet. But something's up. There's double the bunch on the street tonight." He indicated the sidewalk and the throngs of teenagers and young adults, then he let his hand drift to the creeping traffic. "You ever see so many cars, even on a Saturday night?"

"You heard about Matt and Rale?"

"I heard."

GLEN MARKER'S CONFESSION—TAPE

It was dark before either of us made a move to get out of bed. We had gone through three sessions during the afternoon and we both had simply passed out. The only movement of muscle was to pull the satin sheets up over our worn bodies, then our eyes closed and the next thing realized was the darkness of the night and the pounding of traffic on the boulevard outside.

"Prove my point?" grinned Glenda when Cynthia opened her eyes and rolled over.

Cynthia sighed and her hand searched out the instrument of her love-lust beneath the covers. "Honey... Glen... or Glenda, whichever you like best, you can have me any time and in anything you want to wear." She let go of me and rolled over on her back. "Want to go out in drag tonight?"

"Is it safe?"

"I wouldn't suggest it if it wasn't. The cops don't bother the drags much as long as they are minding their own business and the cops aren't just looking for somebody to pick up. Besides, listen to that traffic out there. Friday and Saturday night there are so many on the Strip it would take the whole damned sheriff's force to even start rounding them up. The boys with the long hair have made it easy for your kind."

"Then why not? It's been a long time since I've

had the opportunity. A long time."

"Then you must be starving for it."

Glenda rolled over to look at the girl. "How do you know so much about my kind?"

"There's nothing so tough about that to answer." She turned to look directly at me. "I've had all kinds in my short lifetime. That includes the drags. I told you that before. Of course, I've got to admit the ones who went through with the sex act—and there were few—were never anywhere as good as you, and I don't know any of the straight ones that were as good as you. But I've had the drags around me for years. Clothes are the most important thing to them. Half the time they come up here and I get them all dressed up and first thing you know they're at it by themselves in front of the bedroom mirror over there. What the hell! I get paid! I'm a whore, Glenda. A high-priced one, but a whore no matter how you screw it."

"I wish you wouldn't say that about yourself."

She grinned. "Alright, darling. For you I won't say it again. But you know how I feel. Anyway, about the drags. I never met one yet that wouldn't give his left tit to parade around in drag on the street. That's all there really is in life to them. You may be the best there is in bed, no matter what you wear, but you're no different when it comes to appearing on the street in girls' clothes."

Glenda leaned back on her pillow again. "Well, you have me there. I certainly can't deny that."

"You're really going through with that bit about having yourself changed into a girl like you told me earlier?"

"The minute I get a passport and get going."

"I'll miss you, there's no doubt about that."

"Ships that pass in the night."

"You say the craziest things sometimes."

"I only say what I feel."

"Is that why you said you loved me when we were off on cloud nine this afternoon?"

"Well, you know…"

She laughed delightfully. "Of course I know. I've been on cloud nine too many times to take anything a man says seriously at a time like that. Man! We were gone, gone, gone."

We were silent for a long time. "I'd better get back to the hotel and pick up something to wear if we're going out."

"Why in hell do that? I told you this morning I've got two closets full of clothes and a whole dresser full of everything else. And if you don't like the blonde wig, I've got a brunette and a black one. And I bet my shoes fit too."

"I'd hate to ruin anything of yours, Cynthia."

"Cindy. I like Cindy better. What's to ruin? We're not going with the cocktail gown set. The creeps out there are in capris, or sweaters and skirts, something I've got plenty of."

"You're the boss."

"Unh unh, honey. You are!" and Cynthia reached down under the covers again. "And you're not ready for anything yet."

"I'll tell you one thing I'm ready for."

"Shoot!" She giggled. "Sorry I said that."

"I'm ready for something to eat. I haven't had a thing all day except that whiskey. That only brings on the appetite."

Naked, Cynthia shot out of bed and a moment later Glenda heard the girl moving around some pots and pans. "No sooner said than done!" she shouted back to her before she reached the bedroom door.

Glenda grinned as she heard the light noises from the kitchen, and by the time she had taken a quick shower, Cynthia had a large pan of ham and eggs which she served up. Glenda hadn't bothered to return the nightgown to her body, but she did slip into her own pink panties and a white quilted, satin robe she found on the back of the bathroom door.

We both ate hungrily and almost silently, and when we were finished Cynthia simply piled the dishes in the sink.

"They can wait until later," she said, and opened the belt from around her own robe which she had gotten while I was in the bathroom.

"Always put off today what you can do tomorrow," I grinned as I stood up.

"Only tomorrow never comes." She led the way back into the bedroom. She looked to her watch. "Ten thirty. Things should just about be getting started."

"You're dressing me. What do we wear?"

"That's all according to the mood you're in. Does Glenda wish to be a hard broad, or a soft girl?"

"Glenda has never been a hard broad."

"Blonde? Brunette? Black?"

"Blonde."

"Okay," she replied, then went to the drawers of her dresser and after browsing through it, she came out with a pink angora slip-over sweater.

She put it on a chair, then again turned to the drawer and took out a green angora cardigan.

"Slacks or a skirt?"

"Naturally I prefer a skirt. But for the first time out, slacks or capris."

"Capris we'll have." She took matching pink and matching green capris. "I think you'll like the pink. Do you mind if I go in green?"

"Pink is fine with me."

And it wasn't long before both of us were dressed in the dainty undies and the soft outer sweaters and capris. Cynthia affixed the black wig over her own long hair, and after selecting lightweight matching jackets, we left the apartment.

"What about the elevator boy?"

"What about him? It'll be your test."

I almost grinned at my own question. How many times had I appeared before elevator boys or anyone else for that matter, and had never been questioned? It had been something I thought I should say. And as I had surmised, the only look either of us got from the elevator boy was one of pure fascination, of longing to have either one of us in bed.

We entered upon the crowded Sunset Strip, and Cynthia led our footsteps in the direction of the most action.

"You'll have to do the leading," cooed Glenda. "I haven't the slightest idea about any of the places." We had moved along with a throng of what appeared to be teenagers of both sexes. There was hardly shoulder room between one and the other.

"I've got a few favorites. Not far from here or

we'd have taken my car."

"What good is the car? I like to walk. I like the click of high heels on the cement."

"So do they," Cynthia grinned and indicated three drags in cocktail dresses and fur wraps as they passed us and moved on ahead.

"They're certainly not making any bones about what they are." I grinned as I watched the three gay ones swish broadly along the Boulevard chirping at the top of their lungs.

"Why should they? It's like I told you in the apartment. The cops aren't going to bother them if they don't obviously make a complete ass of themselves by bothering somebody else. But I'm glad you're not the swish kind."

"In my business I couldn't afford to be swish, even if I wanted to be."

"Just what is your business, Glenda?"

"Not now. Sometime perhaps. But not now."

We were quiet a long time, except for occasionally when Cynthia would point out some club which would be of interest to me, or some sight she thought I might want to see. But all in all, her tone became more and more quiet, as if she was sensing something, something laying heavily in the air over the Sunset Strip.

Then, when she was silent for an even greater time, Glenda looked at her. "You're mighty quiet all of a sudden."

"There's something I don't like."

"With me?"

"Of course not, darling. Just something in the air. I don't know what it is yet. But there's something in the air that just doesn't smell kosher tonight. The Strip isn't right tonight!"

"Maybe we'd better hit it back to your place for the night and leave this for another time?"

Glenda was not frightened, but there still was the Dalton Van Carter murder hanging over her head. There would be no doubt but that the Los Angeles Police department would have circulars on the affair. I certainly didn't want to be picked up. They would know within moments who I really was, and even if I got out of the Dalton Van Carter affair, there was always the Syndicate. That's all I needed, was the Syndicate to find out where I was!

"No. We're safer moving with the crowd right now. If something is cooking we'll duck in some place."

"What can be up?"

"This mob is angry. Something feels like it's about to bust loose."

"Then let's get off the street now."

"Alright. Denny's Place is just up ahead." Cynthia pointed to the beer joint which was only two doors along the boulevard. "It's a real gay joint. Nobody's going to bother us there. Most of the 'niks never go in the gay joints. They have their own hangouts."

" 'Niks?"

"Beatniks."

Glenda looked around. "There are plenty of them around."

She took Glenda's arm lightly and we moved into Denny's Place and took a seat in a booth near the rear of the establishment, where across the room an unpleasant looking girl all dressed in red was sipping her first Martini of the evening. Glenda had caught a quick glimpse of the red outfit and remembered his Colorado girlfriend. But that was as far as the recognition went.

CHAPTER FIFTEEN

The Killer in the red dress could hardly keep from choking on the Martini. It was the second night in the bar and there was the prey. Who could miss Glenda? And it was more than convenient. Glenda was wearing angora, her favorite material.

Throughout the day, the Killer had worried about a fact of recognition. What would Glen/Glenda be wearing. Would the make-up be different? Would the wig be changed? Glenda was exactly like her picture, not a hair out of line, and there was the same smile the picture had shown. Pauline had not failed. And the Syndicate would be avenged. Before the night was out, the Killer would have done the job and be back on the airplane and the beloved night-spots of New York.

At no time had the Killer liked the Hollywood scene. If he wanted beatniks he could go to the Village in New York. He didn't have to attend the gay world on the Strip to find them. Soon he would be on his way home to the life he understood, and the people he wanted to be with. It would be so easy to reach into the red plastic purse and take out the small .25 calibre pistol and drive two or three slugs into Glenda's head from that distance. But there were too many others

141

in the bar: the screeching queens and the loud butches, along with the quiet fags. The Killer would have to wait; bide his time. But the opportunity would present itself, and Glenda would be out of this world.

When he realized he would not choke, the Killer slugged down the Martini and slapped a topless waitress on the fanny as she was about to pass him by. It was the same girl he had encountered the night before.

L.A. POLICE INTERVIEW #1212—
SHIRLEY CROSS—TOPLESS WAITRESS—
DENNY'S PLACE.

"Another double?" she asked with her toothy grin.

"Yes." Then a funny thought struck him. He took the girl's arm lightly in his hand before she could turn away. He indicated Glenda and Cynthia across the room from him. "See those two girls over there? The ones in the angora sweaters?"

"Of course."

"You think they're like me?"

Glenda's make-up was perfect. The waitress studied both Glenda and Cynthia from a distance, for a long time. "You must be out of your mind."

"Then what are they doing in a place like this?"

"We get lots of people in here. Gay and otherwise."

"Think they're otherwise?"

"Two girls. Could be the girl lesbian looking

142

for the boy lesbian. We get all kinds in here."

"Give them a drink on me... but don't let them know where it came from."

"It's your money."

The waitress brought the Killer his double Martini, then so as not to tip her hand she went back to her bar and put the other two Martinis on her tray and crossed to Glenda and Cynthia. The Killer grinned silently, unnoticed by anyone else, to himself. He was getting his kicks. He knew his prey, but Glenda didn't have the slightest idea that the vulture was so close.

WARDEN'S NOTE—

The Killer could hardly contain himself, he was that exulted at his good fortune. He wanted to get at his work, and he wanted to get at it soon!

Damn that waitress! Damn the good looks of Glenda! Glenda could fool anybody, but a damned fool waitress could see through him. The Killer didn't like any part of that. The Killer wanted the pretty Glenda off the face of the earth. He wanted Glenda found on the street or in an alley, and when the morgue people lifted the skirt and took down the panties, there would be more than revenge. He only wished he didn't have to kill Glenda outright. Just wound her a little so that the cops or the nurses would add the final touch of embarrassment. Glenda had never been found out. Damn her to hell!

The Killer finished off the second double in one gulp, but he kept Glenda and Cynthia in the corner of his eye. He would not remove them from his vision if his life depended upon it. He knew his life did depend upon it.

He ordered and got another Martini. The darkness of the small joint blurred his eyes at times, but he wasn't going to let the effects of any alcohol cheat him out of his fun. But he wanted another, and another. He cursed the two girls silently because they were staying too long. He wanted them on the street where he could use the gun, or the switchblade knife which was also in the purse. He bided his time in the interesting thoughts just as to which he would use—the gun or knife. How very much he would like to get close enough to Glenda and look her in her beautiful eyes and slit the knife directly between the perfect falsies. He bided his time in the thought of how the sponge rubber of the falsies would soak up the blood, and how he wished he could have one or even both of them for souvenirs...

Which would it be? The knife or the gun? Only time and the opportunity would give him the answer to that. If it was the knife, it would find its way directly between those phoney tits. If it was the gun, then there was only one place Glenda would get it. Right in the head. Two or three quick ones right in the head...

L.A. POLICE INTERVIEW #1212—
SHIRLEY CROSS—TOPLESS WAITRESS—
DENNY'S PLACE

The Killer giggled to himself as the waitress brought him another double Martini. "You're giggling, " she said. "That's a dead giveaway."

"You mind your own business!" The Killer's

eyes grew hard. He could just as well send that girl into the unknown along with Glenda. But he changed his tone almost immediately. "What did they say? Those two girls I sent the booze over to?"

"Not much."

"I didn't ask you that. I asked you what they said?"

"Of course, they wanted to know who sent the stuff."

"And you said?"

"An admirer. That's all. Just somebody who liked them, and the girl in the green angora sweater told the other one she thought one of the lesbians at the bar was trying to make out. You know. I think if they decide to put their mind to it, they will make out."

The Killer's face twisted in anger again and the girl knew she was in for a bruise if she stayed in his vicinity, so she turned and hurried back toward the bar.

WARDEN'S NOTE—

How dare they speak of lesbians, was all that suddenly raced through the Killer's mind. He'd give them the lesbian bit! After all, didn't he appear to be a girl? They could have him anytime they wanted. It wouldn't be such a bad idea getting Glenda in bed with him for a time before he used the knife between those perfect phonies. Glenda might give quite a good session. She must have given that Dalton Van Carter quite a session. No one got close enough to Dalton Van Carter to kill him unless they are damned good in bed.

"The bitch!" screamed the Killer silently into his fresh Martini. "She'd take one look at me and I'd only be a piece of dirt to her, the rotten bitch! Her and her pretty face. I love girls' clothes just as much as she does. Where does the bitch get off thinking she's prettier than me? Wouldn't have a date with me, would she? Well I don't want no date with her either. I came out here to kill her and that's what's going to be done! Kill her and she'll never know what hit her, and she'll never know I even thought of giving her the benefit of my body. She'll go out never knowing I existed." He emptied the glass again and the waitress quickly slipped another in front of him and retreated. The Killer toyed with the stem of the glass and his mind's eye could conjure up in a reflection of Glenda and the pink angora sweater in the clear liquid. "Too bad that beautiful sweater has to get bloodstained. I wish I could get her where she'd have to take it off. I'd do what I did so long ago. I'd dress in those beautiful pink things and I'd give her one hell of a jazzin', and when she was about to pop the stem, I'd blast her right between the eyes. The queer bitch... that's what I'd do. I'd strip her right down and make her look at it in the mirror. I'd make her die looking at the male body she really is. That would be the thing that would put the fear of horror in her guts. Make her die like the boy she really is. I wouldn't even let her look at any girls' clothes while she died, unless they were on me. Then I would let her look..." The Killer slopped a good portion of the Martini over the table as he traveled it toward his lips.

CHAPTER SIXTEEN

Terry eased the police patrol car in toward the curb near Denny's Place, then stopped, but kept the motor running. "They're out for blood tonight," he mumbled as he surveyed the milling mobs of teenagers mixed with the beatnik groups.

"Think that's what it is, Terry?"

"It's the only thing it can be. Look at that mob over on the corner... over there." He pointed. "You ever seen them around the Strip before tonight?"

Gilboy looked the group over carefully. "That's a new bunch to me."

Terry changed the direction of his pointing finger several times more. "And there. And there....over there. It's the same way along the whole mile and a half. Last night's action clinches it as far as I'm concerned." He paused and lifted his radiophone, but for the moment did not snap it on. "We tag any one of them tonight and I hate to think what will happen."

"Like in Watts?"

"Like in Watts. Maybe worse."

"Can anything be worse?"

"Before this night is over we may damned

147

well find out. I don't like what I feel... and I damned well don't like what I see."

"These kids usually mind the police when they're told to do something."

"The kids, maybe. But not the toughs you see around here. Lot of the kids in Watts used to mind the police too. But when the riot started, everybody got into the act." He snapped on the radiophone and when headquarters cleared in, he said: "Let me talk to the Chief."

There was a long silent wait as Terry refused to take his eyes from the sidewalk and the crowd. Then the Chief came on the wire. "What's up, Terry?"

"I smell riot weather, Claude."

"You sure?"

"Just as sure as I can be, before something actually starts it all off. That's pretty sure on my part."

"I'll get more men in the field right away."

"That would be my advice. From where I sit looking out the windshield, I'd say we have an imported load of professionals."

"As bad as that?"

"I had the same feeling in Watts when we went down to help out the local department."

Claude buzzed off a moment, then came back on the wire. "Okay. I gave the order. The men will be on the street in five minutes. I'll ride car sixteen if you want me."

"See you on the street of dreams," Terry quipped as he snapped off the receiver and hung it back into place. He looked to Gilboy. "Where's your pistol?"

"Under the sweatshirt." He lifted the sweatshirt to reveal the handle of the snub-nosed .38.

"Keep it handy." Then Terry reached under the seat. He handed Gilboy two apple-shaped objects. "You might need some tear-gas. Use it rather than your gun unless the gun becomes absolutely necessary. There are always a few innocent citizens who get mixed up in these things. I'd hate to have them spend Sunday in the hospital—or the morgue."

"Okay, Terry."

"You have a sap?"

"Lined in along the back of my belt."

"Get it clear. Put it in your side pocket where you can get at it mighty damned quick. You might have to crack some skulls before they can crack yours." His eyes narrowed as he looked across the street to another bunch who were ambling around the corner of Laurel Canyon to enter upon the Sunset Strip. "Those are pros. They know what it's all about. When things start it's not going to be easy." Terry looked ahead to the almost bumper to bumper traffic. "Another smart move. They're moving in the heavy line of defense; the vehicle traffic, bumper to bumper so our boys can't get their squad cars through in a hurry."

"What happens if our boys can't get through?"

"Oh, I don't think we have too much to worry about on that score. There are too many lead-in streets to the Strip. They can't block them all. They block the entire length of the Strip and we still have a couple of dozen lead-in streets from headquarters. Most of this thing is going to be done on foot anyway if it is to be done at all."

Suddenly Terry's eyes shot to the right of his

car, past Gilboy. "There it comes."

Gilboy snapped his eyes in that direction also. Two sets of four bearded beatniks each stood facing each other. It was apparent hot words were flying at each other. "That's for our benefit," shouted Terry. "But we've got to take them. Watch both sides. They want us, not each other."

Gilboy snapped open his door at the same instant Terry threw open his, and both men raced across the sidewalk. Two uniformed men seemed to appear from nowhere and joined Terry and Gilboy just as they reached the gang. The uniformed men quickly permitted Terry to take the initiative. "Okay, okay. Break it up and move along!"

"Or what, cop?" shouted the bearded leader.

"Just snap it up or you'll be inside looking out."

A young man with hair hanging well below his shoulders snapped up and looked to Gilboy. "Look, gang! The creep that's been hangin' 'round the joints. Fuzz in sheep's clothing. Spies they got yet!"

Gilboy stepped up beside Terry. "You heard what the sergeant told you."

The leader put defiant hands on his hips. "No, what did the sergeant say, fuzz?"

Terry grabbed the leader and spun him violently across the sidewalk until he hit the side of the squad car. "Get into position. You know the one I mean."

Long Hair took two, three quick steps across the sidewalk and roughly grabbed Terry by the arm in an effort to spin him around. "You take

150

your hands off him, fuzz!"

But Terry didn't spin so easily. His elbow shot backward and caught Long Hair just below the rib-cage. The breath escaped through the man's gaping mouth and he went down on both knees with both his hands frantically pumping at his stomach, pumping violently to replace the escaping air, a futile exercise at least.

One victory does not mean the battle won. The victory in that case was only the beginning. The hordes came in from all sides in one screaming Indian charge. It was Custer and the Sioux all over again. Police whistles sounded from all ends. Another bunch of 'niks which raced across the Boulevard from the direction of Laurel Canyon came swinging tire irons. The fenders on stalled cars fell quickly to their mercy and the windshields crashed under the iron blows.

A bus, stopped by the wall of traffic, became the target for a torch-swinging youth who hopped its tailgate.

A sloppy, bearded youth pulled a sweater-and-skirt clad girl whom he had been following, into a darkened doorway and ripped off her skirt while in the same motion he unzipped his fly and was taking her before she could let out the first scream. Scream or not, she couldn't be heard or distinguished from any of the other screams, and the screams of sirens as police cars tried to break through.

Hopelessly outnumbered, Terry and his men put their backs against the squad car and faced the tearing mob with nightclubs, then he shouted. "Let them have it, Gilboy!"

The young officer pulled the pin and let the

tear-gas bomb sail into the midst of the charging mob. It stopped them for a brief moment, but none of the officers were dumb enough to think it would break them up for more than a minute; just long enough for them to regroup and come in from another direction.

Every block of the area found itself experiencing the same destructive forces. Headlights smashed quickly, in violent succession to any with a heavy object in their hand. Nothing was safe or sacred to the mob of maniacs... the call was out. "Kill the fuzz! You want freedom? Kill the fuzz! Kill every last one of them!"

And they tried. They came at the men of the department with everything they could wield or throw. The more helmeted officers who joined in the melee, the more vicious the mob became. Then an automobile was overturned onto the sidewalk from the parking place at the curb. Another girl screamed as she was tossed to the ground and her dress ripped off. She was quickly lifted and secreted away by three cursing thugs. But still not a shot had been fired.

Terry knew the professional rioters had guns in their possession and he expected the bullets to fly at any moment. But they held off, seemingly satisfied with the destructive forces at their command with the heavy weapons they held in hand.

He knew it couldn't last. The taste of blood was in their mouths and until they drank of human flesh they would not be satisfied. Whoever was behind the riot had picked their best men. They knew their business.

In the end Terry and his department would

win. But to what end would that win attest?

The screams in the night turned to cries of pain. All the pent-up emotion of the non-professionals suddenly let go. It was no longer a fight among the thugs and the police. It was a mass of swinging fists and weighted objects. It no longer mattered who was hit, as long as the hit connected with something or someone.

Terry realized then, it was the beginning of the end.

CHAPTER SEVENTEEN

GLEN MARKER'S CONFESSION— TAPE

Cynthia and I, long before the riot started, had a good laugh when we were served the Martinis by our unknown admirer. But neither of us were reluctant to take then. We thanked the waitress and then turned to watch where she went next. For the moment it did us little good, because she simply went back to the bar and waited around for another order.

"I think it would be funny," grinned Cynthia.

"You're having a joke you're not letting me in on."

"I was just thinking if it was some lez who sent the drinks over, what fun it would be to let her come over to the table, and after a time she'd start groping you. What a surprise!" And she laughed harder.

"What makes you think it would be a lez?"

"None of the boys in here would go for you or me. Only other boys. After all, darling, we are two very beautiful girls. Soft and cuddly and all that sort of thing."

Glenda kept her eyes on the waitress for a long time and saw the skinny girl in red ordering Martini after Martini. Several times Glenda was sure the girl in red was looking across to them, but she waited sometime before she mentioned it.

"You think so?" smiled Cynthia, trying to look out of the corner of her eye.

"She keeps looking in this direction."

"I can't get a good look at her."

"Don't bother. It's about the ugliest drag I've seen in all my life."

"You're sure it's a drag?"

"As sure as I've ever been about anything."

"What in hell would another drag want with a couple of dolls like us?" Cynthia tried to brush the thought out of her mind.

"Maybe he's double-gaited. Then again, perhaps he's just another transvestite like I am... looking for a score."

"No matter what. At least we got a free drink out of him. We just don't pay any attention." She sipped of her Martini.

But it bothered Glenda. Something about the drag in red gave her a creepy feeling in her stomach. Glenda didn't like the feeling. She wanted to get up from the table and confront the little bastard, then jam her fist into his ugly face.

But what the hell? "I suppose he's got as much a right to look around for a score as anyone else," she said silently, then saluted Cynthia with the glass and also drank.

Glenda tried to shake the creature from her mind with the thought, but it didn't work that way. A creepy stomach was hard to shake, and a creepy stomach didn't come unless there was some cause for it. The way Cynthia had felt something wrong on the Strip outside was the same way Glenda felt about the girl in red who continually sneaked her looks at them. She had felt the same feelings many times when she was

155

with the Syndicate, and there the creepy stomach took a deep turn. It was the same feelings she had had when she watched the Syndicate at work all those years she had been with it.

She couldn't believe her own thoughts, that they could be onto her; they could know where she had gone. But she couldn't dismiss that feeling in her stomach so easily. It was there, and it was that power of disaster—ultimate, pending disaster.

"Let's get out of here, Cynthia."

"In a little while. I still have that feeling about out there on the Strip."

"Well, I have a little feeling about being in here right now, love."

She looked at her strangely. "Do you smell cop?"

"I don't know what I smell, but whatever it is, I don't like it one damned bit. If you don't want to go out on the Strip, is there a back door we can get out of?"

Her eyes narrowed. "Are you in some kind of trouble?"

"Whatever it is, I don't want you getting mixed up in it. Let's just get out of here."

Before either of them could stand up the first blast of many sirens criss-crossed on sound waves across the room. The sound snapped them momentarily back into their seats. Their eyes raced toward the front door which Denny had thrown open. Then just as quickly he closed it, threw on the lock, and put an iron bar into place as extra security. He looked to the half-empty interior.

"Don't nobody get excited. It looks like the

Strip is another Watts!" he shouted.

The information sent a shudder through everyone in the place and many of the queens went into panic. Denny held up his hand again for their silence and to give his orders. "Now you're plenty safe in here if you don't go out on the street. But if you want to leave, take it easy and go out the back way. Go across the parking lot and down the hill. Just do yourself a favor and keep off the Strip proper. They've gone mad out there, all up and down the street."

He then raced behind the bar and poured himself a stiff jolt, looked to the door where it appeared someone was trying to force their way in, then jolted himself again with a double shot.

"Do we go or stay?" asked Cynthia, a bit of panic beginning to show in her own face.

"We go." I indicated the back. "Out the back way like the man said."

"We'll have to hit the Strip sooner or later to get to my place. I'm right in the middle of it."

"Not tonight we won't. We'll grab the first cab we can find on one of the other streets and get as far away from here as we can go with the cash you have in your purse. My wallet is back at your place."

"I've got enough."

Glenda lost most of her feminine traits as she took hold of Cynthia's arm and raced with her to the back door which was situated in a small hallway between the men's and ladies' can. The cool air rushed into their faces along with the smell of burning rubber. The mob had set fire to the bus and an overturned car, which they could see through the alleyway between Denny's place and the next building. Glenda didn't permit much of a look. She hustled Cynthia across the parking lot, and the first bullet tore up the grass just at the edge of the parking lot.

Cynthia stopped dead in her tracks and twisted her head back toward the bar. "That was a shot."

"Just keep moving!" screamed Glenda in a higher pitched tone than she had mustered since her high school days.

"But somebody's shooting at us."

"Good Christ, do as I tell you!" Glenda had seen the skinny tramp in red racing across the parking lot after them. Glenda twisted Cynthia's arm violently and the girl flew off balance. She toppled down the steep, grassy incline, and in the move, she shot out with her arm and grabbed Glenda's sweater front. They both rolled head over heels down the slope and only came to a stop when they had found the bottom.

Glenda didn't wait for any explanations. She bodily lifted Cynthia to her feet and pushed her toward a car which was parked on the side street. The second bullet tore into the hood of the car just as they ducked down behind it.

"Somebody *is* shooting at us!"

"And don't I know it. Keep your head down."

"Why are we being singled out?" Cynthia found the first dark tears of hysteria flooding her eyes.

"*We* aren't being singled out. I am. You're in it only because they've caught up with me while you're along."

"They? They who?"

"The Syndicate, damn it."

"What has the Syndicate got to do with you?"

"I broke with them earlier this year. They've been after me all the time. Damn! I should have known they'd use a drag to search me out. I've been stupid. For the first time in my life I've played it stupid. Where else would they look for me but in a gay bar? Who else would they send after me but another drag? What's one more drag in a drag bar?"

The next shot tore through the pink angora and into Glenda's left shoulder. The blood splattered up and down her front and onto the front fender of the automobile, their protection. The shock of the slug spun Glenda into the street. But all the reflexes were still there. Glenda spun to the protection. Cynthia screamed once, then jammed her fist into her own mouth to keep from screaming again. The pain was violent in Glenda's shoulder, but she fought stiffly to keep her senses. She lowered her head behind the hood again, and sneaked a look around the front of the car.

The Killer in the red dress stood out in the open, just a few yards in front of us. There was no hiding from the Killer. He knew his opponents had no weapons.

"He only wants me." Glenda spoke in a low whisper.

Cynthia didn't take her fist from her mouth, but she whimpered. "Don't leave me. Oh, please don't leave me."

"I've got to do something, or we're both going to be killed. I've got to talk to him." Glenda leaned partially around the hood of the car and called. "You! Can we talk?"

Glenda snapped her head around the hood again just as a piece of searing lead took off a headlight. "You only want me fella, why don't you let the girl go? She doesn't even know what you look like."

"Go ahead. Beg! I like that."

"I'll do anything you want. Just let the girl go! The Syndicate don't want her. They only want me."

"Pretty little thing, so you've always thought. You know, when I was coming up in the ranks of the Syndicate, I looked at you as my kind of idol. I never thought I'd see my idol on his knees."

"I'll get on my knees for you. Just let the girl go."

"Back in the bar I was thinking how beautiful you are and how ugly I am. I got to thinking how there isn't a drag in the world that wants to die naked, where he can see, and show the rest of the world how he's only a male in female clothes. I think that's about the most horrible death any of us, our kind, could think of. You're not going to die with your clothes on, Glenda. You're going to die naked as a jaybird. And if you've ruined that pink sweater I'm going to give you slugs in both eyes. The fates have been kind to me tonight, putting you and me in the same place at the same time, and with a riot to cover for me. It gives me the opportunity to finish you off the way I want. You were always the love of the underworld. I was nothing. *I'll* be pretty when you die."

Glenda's throat went dry. She knew the score. She had never expected to die as the male she had come into the world. Perhaps the clothing would only have been an illusion, but it would have been the way she wanted it. The Killer knew how to torture. And it looked like there was nothing she could do about it.

"Let the girl go! I'll come out. I'll make it easy for you. Easy all the way. Anything you want."

"He'll kill you," Cynthia cried.

"He's got us in a spot. Who knows? Maybe I'll get the breaks." Glenda reached over and kissed Cynthia swiftly. "As soon as I tell you, you beat it off down the road. That's only a .25 pistol he's got. It's only good at close range. When I tell you to run, you Goddamned well run. And take those high heels off now. You only have to make it ten or twelve steps and you'll be out of range. Head for the Strip. He'll never find you in that mess up there. The Strip may turn out to be the safest place on earth for you tonight. Now, you got it straight?"

"Coming out, bright eyes?" The Killer was becoming impatient. Glenda knew she didn't have much time to make a decision.

"I don't want to leave you."

"You've got to, Cynthia. That's a killer out there."

"I'll get the police. I'll send them back."

"Fine! You do that!" Glenda knew it would be too late, but Cynthia was so near panic she didn't want to worry her any further. "You get up there and get the cops back here."

Cynthia kicked off her shoes and prepared herself at the rear end of the car as Glenda had told her.

"Now don't take off until I shout at you to run.

161

I've got to cover for you to give you that extra moment or two."

Cynthia nodded her head. She couldn't speak. The tears were closing off her voice.

"Good girl," Glenda whispered, then loudly: "I'm coming out. Just leave the girl alone."

Glenda stood up. For a moment she thought about raising her hands. But what the hell good would that do? The Killer had a slug for her no matter what she did.

"Just move forward slowly. Nice and easy. I want to watch you undress. Then I want to watch you die. You want your girlfriend to get out of this, you do just like you're told!"

Glenda moved forward slowly. She caught a last glimpse of Cynthia crouched by the rear wheel and she knew the girl was ready; and she knew Cynthia would take her orders. When she would shout to her, Cynthia would run. She had to shout that order at precisely the right moment. Glenda knew the Killer had no intentions of letting the girl go free. It would have to be Glenda who made the move which would give Cynthia the chance.

Glenda stopped two feet from the ugly Killer who smiled until the wet saliva of lust drooled at the corners of his lips. Somewhere during the run the Killer had lost his wig, and without it he was more ugly than ever.

"You got a good look?"

"I got a good look!"

"And what do you see, my pretty?"

"I don't think you want to hear."

"Take the sweater off!"

Glenda slipped the sweater up over her head

and held it in her hands. She wore no slip, but the brassiere with its rubber padding stood out beautifully in the half light.

"I even thought of putting a knife between your falsies. I don't think I'll do that. I'd have to get too close to you. We can't take any chances like that, can we? You do have pretty titties though, even if they are falsies. Another time, I could really go for you."

"Get it over with."

"Your girl still back there?"

"You didn't see her go, did you?"

"I wonder if she is *really* a girl." The Killer lifted his voice. "You hear that back there? I wonder if you are a real girl. Maybe our boy up here is double-gaited." He laughed. "I asked you what you saw?"

Glenda narrowed her eyes hard. It was now or never. She had to make the first move count. "I see a no-good son of a bitch that wouldn't make a good wart on a homosexual's belly!"

Glenda had almost been too late. At the same time the gun spoke and the bullet drove itself into a small space just below her heart, Glenda screamed "Run, Cindy!" and threw the pink angora sweater directly into the creep's face. But the Killer automatically spun toward the racing footsteps, and although blinded by the sweater which momentarily covered his face, he fired two quick shots.

There was no time to think of pain or anything else. Glenda flew forward. The bullet sound just under her heart tore open even wider by the sudden force against it. But she hit the mark. Glenda was no longer Glenda. The wound tore open, the

163

wig flew from my head.

I was all powerful; there was no force on earth which could keep me from my attack. The startled Killer let out one quick scream and went to the ground under my pure dead weight.

My fist smashed out and I felt the teeth break and the sudden rawness as my knuckles tore open. I felt the gun butt or barrel, I couldn't distinguish which, slam into the side of my neck and I saw the stars of the sky all in one glorious blast! But my hand locked over the gun, and it couldn't fire. My other hand, bloody with my life's blood, clenched around the gun wrist like a vice. It seemed an eternity until my bleary eyes could see the small pistol turning, ever turning, until the barrel was firmly against the Killer's chin.

The Killer had time for only one scream, and even that was chopped off in the middle as the gun spoke, to blow the man's jaw through the top of his head.

I saw the man's last breath rush out of what once had been his throat in a great bubble of blood. Then I rolled over, off the dead man in the red drag, and I let the cool grass melt into my back. I hurt more than I had ever hurt in all my life. There didn't seem to be a spot on my whole body which didn't burn with all the fires of hell.

And 'hell' caused me to wonder—was that where I was going? A lot of the figures of my own victims crossed my vision. Then for a long moment everything went black. But the blood in my mouth, sticky sweet, brought me back to consciousness again. My eyes looked up to the dark heavens where the stars twinkled. Some of the smoke from burning buildings and cars on the Strip crossed the sky high above me, but I could see the stars. There didn't seem to be anything which could blot the stars from my view just then. They were there and they were bright.

Another spasm sent the blood rushing from my wounds and up through my mouth. I couldn't move any longer, not even my arms or my hands. Such simple little movements I had done all my life; there were none, and I knew that I'd had it. I felt the end was close, but I fought for every precious second of it.

There was no longer movement and there was no longer any voice I could command. Only the sounds of violence somewhere, a long way from me. Only the sounds of violence which should have comforted me in my dying moments.

I had lived by and with violence all my life. Strange it would be such a violence that I would hear in the last seconds. It was as if it were violence that was singing my swansong. It was violence that had come from nowhere to see me off, to bid me adieu, to exit me from the only world I had ever known.

Everything suddenly seemed so silly to me. The whole scheme of things. I wanted to laugh, but I couldn't focus my senses to even that privilege. I was not to be permitted even that last movement toward fate. But I did realize I was still in drag. I would die in the clothes I had always hoped for. I only wished I could reach the angora sweater and the wig. But I had outwitted the Killer. The Killer was not to see me die with or without the clothes of my choice. It was the one glowing thought.

Then I heard Cynthia's scream, and I knew she had returned. Perhaps Cynthia would see I was buried as I would have wanted. There was plenty of money for such a thing in my wallet at her apartment.

What a strange thought, I realized as the blackness closed in.

CHAPTER EIGHTEEN

EPILOG TO FATE

Glenda had long since slipped into pink nylon panties, brassiere and slip. Over it she wore a brown skirt, frilly white blouse and a brown cashmere cardigan sweater. Even the brown, high-heeled shoes fitted comfortably. And as she finished her story, she put a cigarette between her freshly painted lips and waited for Charlie to light it. She took the burning cigarette from her lips and her eyes grew bright at seeing the smear of fresh lipstick on the end. Such a small thing, but so powerful in its meaning during those last few minutes. There was the sexual lust she had always felt, but which Glenda had been denied for so many months, yet there was nothing to be done for release. She wanted a full-length mirror—there was none.

She leaned back on the cot with a feeling of great relief creeping over her entire body. She hugged her arms tightly around her, her fingers digging deep into the soft pile of the sweater. Her eyes fluttered rapidly, girlishly, as she looked across to the slowly spinning tape recorder, then on to Charlie, and finally to myself, as I leaned against the holding cell bars, my arms folded.

"This really is the only thing I regret having to leave, the feeling of it all." Glenda stroked the soft wool lovingly. She looked back to Charlie.

"Your daughter has excellent taste, Uncle Charlie. Tell her so for me. Tell her, from the skin out, she has excellent taste."

Charlie nodded.

Glenda came forward on the cot. "So the record has spun its measured spin. The story is told. The Sunset Strip fuzz sped me to a hospital where I eventually came around. My fingerprints, taken as strictly routine while I was unconscious, were checked out and I was found to be wanted back here. One thing led to another and here I am—and here I end." Glenda took her hands from caressing the soft sweater long enough to shrug her narrow shoulders. "That's about the whole story as I lived it."

I was puzzled. "But you committed no crime out on the coast. Why the secrecy all this time about your moves?"

Glenda laughed her musical laugh. She indicated her lovely clothing. "I wonder if I would have gotten these things if I had no story to tell." This time her cigarette was crushed out on the cement floor by the pointed toe of her high-heeled shoe. "But, Warden, you should be able to see now why it is so important to a transvestite not to leave this world in male attire. It's our religion, so to speak. Maybe we live a lie, but also perhaps in death we have come to a truth. Are you sorry we made our bargain?"

I left my position at the bars, then crossed to turn off the tape recorder. Finally I looked back to the beautiful Glenda. "A bargain is a bargain. I always keep my word." Then I slammed my fist into an open palm. "Damn... I look at you and I see a vision of loveliness who could have done so much with your talents. I have little doubt but that you could have made it big on the stage; maybe even in the movies. Certainly, a fine-looking girl as you present, you'd have made it as a girl in any walk of life you desired..."

Glenda grinned. "I did, Warden. I did make it as a girl—in the profession of my choice. And I made it big."

I looked around the bleak cell. "Sure you did. Right into the big house."

Charlie the guard looked to his wrist-watch then nudged me as he again indicated his watch. Glenda caught the action and knew. A strange sensation of loneliness crept swiftly through her body, a sudden realization of the finality in her situation. Even so long ago, laying on the ground with bullet holes exposing the inside of her body to the elements, there had been only a feeling of deep relaxation. There had been no feeling of finality. Nothing like that which she experienced in those last moments. The exactness of the end came in an overpowering cloak of fear which shook her entire frame. She hugged her arms tighter around her body again, only this time it was for more than the feel of the female softness. She fought down the shakes which were nearly uncontrollable. She didn't want the shakes. She didn't want any of us to see she had any fear. She had watched so many others tremble at the sight of her gun, she didn't want anyone to think she could not take what she dished out.

Glenda spoke softly in an attempt to hide her trembling tones. "About that time?"

I closed and locked the lid of the tape recorder. "Seven minutes."

"Seven minutes to eternity." Glenda didn't want to even think about it, let alone say the words. But they had come out through slack lips.

"The people you took never had seven minutes to think about anything." It had been the first hard words I had uttered throughout the entire interview.

"But they never knew—until the last second. It's better that way. Not knowing. Knowing the precise moment, the waiting, that's the real punishment in a thing like this."

I lifted the tape recorder and handed it to a uniformed guard who put it on the floor outside of the cell. "There is still time if you want to see the Padre."

Glenda stood up. She straightened the front of her cardigan, then made sure it was laying neatly over the top of her skirt.

"I'm wearing my religion," she said softly. Then as an afterthought she let one hand drift to the spot on her head which had been shaved. "I hate to have my public see me with this. Always before I've had the most beautiful wigs." She looked at me and tried for a weak smile. " Forgive me for looking backward, Warden. But since it appears I have so little future, I can only remember what was in the past."

"Feel it as you see best, Glen."

"Please... Glenda." She made the appropriate gesture.

"Yes... Glenda."

Glenda let her hands once more caress along the smooth lines of her brown skirt. "Well, are there any more preparations? We want everything to go off just as it should."

I shook my head and Glenda got that sinking look again. Momentarily she thought her legs would buckle beneath her. She braced the back of her legs against the cot for added support. It was of little help against the dizziness which swam in her head and blurred her eyes.

"Will you need help?"

Glenda forced a partial clearing to her eyes as she looked to me. There was no doubt then about the trembling in her voice. "No! I'll be alright. There are times a lady must walk unaided. Just give me a minute... I'll be alright."

"Time is running out. If you have to be helped..."

I made a sign with my hand and one of the uniformed guards started through the cell doors. "There are no more minutes." I was firm.

It was evident Glenda had no intentions of being aided by anyone for the last short walk of her life. There would be the witnesses and there would be representatives of the press. They would not print Glenda Satin/Glen Marker had to be carried to the chair. That was something none of them were going to get a chance to print. And the thought seemed to give her renewed strength. The power returned to her legs. Suddenly the high heels were firm under her feet again. The strength steadily grew throughout her body until she stood straight and tall. Once more she flounced up the frills on her blouse and again straightened the sweater over the skirt top. The guard had stopped in the cell doorway.

She would now be a lady all the way and prove it. The press would remember her for a long time to come.

Glenda walked out of the cell, unaided, to take her place in the center position of four uniformed guards. I took up my place at the head of the column and Charlie fell to the rear. We stepped off at an extremely slow pace, our steps steadily moving toward a green steel door.

*****

One of the reporters in the witness-stand watched the beautiful, short-haired girl mince her way toward the seat of destruction. He wanted to whistle, but instead turned to a fellow reporter.

"I thought it was a guy they were strapping in..."

—THE END—